THE ROBOT GOD
AND OTHER STRANGE CREATIONS

THE ROBOT GOD

AND OTHER STRANGE CREATIONS

RAY CUMMINGS

WILDSIDE PRESS

"The Robot God" was first published in *Weird Tales*, July 1941. "The Flame Breathers" was first published in *Planet Stories*, March 1943. "Space-Flight of Terror" was first published in *Science Fiction*, January 1941. "The Thought Machine" was first published in *Argosy All-Story Weekly*, May 26, 1923. "The Curious Case of Norton Hoorne" was first published *Argosy All-Story Weekly*, April 2, 1921.

Published by Wildside Press LLC.
wildsidepress.com | bcmystery.com

CONTENTS

INTRODUCTION

To anyone interested in the roots of modern science fiction, the name of Ray Cummings (1887–1957) should already be well known. He wrote at the dawn of the science fiction field, publishing genre stories in mainstream magazines like *Argosy*, *Munsey's Magazine*, and other top publications of the day. The editor fo *Argosy-All Story Weekly* dubbed him "The American H.G. Wells." Of course, as soon as the science fiction pulp magazines debuted, he moved to them, where his work received a hearty welcome from fans. He continued publishing through the 1950s.

Cummings was born in New York City. He worked with Thomas Edison as a personal assistant and technical writer from 1914 to 1919, which provided much background for his fiction. His most famous work remains the novel *The Girl in the Golden Atom*, first published in 1922. It combined a short story by the same name first published in 1919 (in which he merged themes from Fitz James O'Brien's novel *The Diamond Lens* with H. G. Wells's *The Time Machine*). Its sequel, *The People of the Golden Atom*, appeared in 1920.

During the 1940s, with his literary career in decline—his work was decidedly old-fashioned in comparison to that of Asimov, Heinlein, van Vogt, and the other new authors—Cummings found himself relegated to second-tier science fiction magazines. He began to turn to comic books for a market, and he soon found work writing for Timely Comics, the predecessor to Marvel Comics. In those days, comics appealed to a much younger and far less sophisticated audience. For Timely, he recycled the plot of *The Girl in the Golden Atom* as a two-part Captain America tale, "Princess of the Atom" (*Captain America Comics* #25 and #26). He also contributed stories featuring the Human Torch and Sub-Mariner, sometimes in collaboration with his daughter, Betty Cummings (who also wrote comics scripts by herself, often using her father's more famous name). Ray Cummings also began to write mysteries, often with a science-based or fantastic twist.

Though largely forgotten today, his work remains interesting for its place in the history of science fiction.

—John Betancourt
Cabin John, Maryland

THE ROBOT GOD

CHAPTER 1

Voyage of Doom

To young George Carter the girl seemed more beautiful tonight than he had ever seen her. The shine of spacelight was in her eyes— soft pale-blue glow of the million million starry worlds. It filtered down through the overhead glassite dome of the little space-liner, bathing him and her in its soft effulgence.

" 'Flinging back a million starglints,' " he quoted softly, " 'the depths of space remind me of thine eyes.' That's literally true, to-night, Dierdre."

The *Starfield Queen* was a day out from Earth on its voyage to Ferrok Shahn, capital of the Martian Union. By Earth-time it was August, 2453 A.D. By ship's routine the time could be called mid-evening—an hour or two after the passengers and crew of the little liner had had their evening meal. Still within the giant cone of the Earth's shadow the great black firmament blazed with its myriad white worlds. It was an awe-inspiring sight to Carter—his first voy-age out of the Earth's stratosphere. He was a big, rather handsome blond fellow in his early twenties. An Anglo-American Mining chemist; and his company was sending him now on a prospecting trip to Mars.

The girl laughed; a little ripple of silver laughter. But to Carter, somehow it seemed forced. He had known Dierdre Dynne about a year. She was traveling now to Mars with her father; only by chance had they both taken this voyage on the *Starfield Queen*.

And there was something, now, about her that was abnormal. He had noticed it at once. A restlessness; a vague uneasiness?

He stared into her blue eyes, where the starshine was mirrored. Was it terror there, glowing in the limpid depths? They were on the upper deck of the hundred foot spaceship—an oblong space on the superstructure roof, with the glassite pressure dome close over them. Behind them, beyond the stern-peak, the great dull-red ball of Earth, with the cone of its giant shadow streaming out here from it, filled a quadrant of the heavens.

For a moment silent, he gazed at Dierdre, who was stretched beside him in her padded deck chair. Slim, beautiful little figure in gray-blue traveling trousers, blue blouse with white neck ruff; and her blond hair, pale as spun gold, braided and coiled on her head. The small platinum ornaments that dangled from her bare arms clinked as with nervous fingers she toyed with them.

He said suddenly, "What's the matter with you, Dierdre?"

"Matter with me?"

It was terror in her eyes. No question of it now. He leaned toward her. The little starlit deck space up here at the moment seemed empty—a few deck chairs scattered about, and squat metal vents of the ventilators and air-pressure mechanisms. No one seemed here. But he lowered his voice.

"Something is worrying you," he insisted. And then he smiled. "All right—but I asked you a while ago and you didn't answer. Why are you and your father going to Mars?"

Her jeweled hand went out and touched his arm. "I guess I—will tell you, George," she murmured. She was suddenly breathless. "You know, of course—these last few years, several space-liners have vanished. Just—never heard of again—"

Five passenger ships, enroute between Earth, Venus and Mars, mysteriously had been lost. He knew that, of course. Little space-vehicles in commercial service—like this *Starfield Queen*—equipped with radio-helio and every modern safety device—just vanishing. And now, of course she was timid, here on her first voyage—

"Oh," he said. "Well, I don't blame you. But nothing is going to happen to us."

"No, it's more than that, George. Father's on his way to Ferrok Shahn to consult with some of the Martian Robot Manufacturer's. You see, what you don't know—what naturally has never been made public—"

* * * *

He stared, silent, as she told him. Her father, Dr. Ely Dynne, was a retired Robot Manufacturer. A man in his sixties now; and it was his genius which had developed these weird mechanisms in the guise of humans. The Dynne domestic-servant robots were known throughout all three of the inhabited worlds. Amazing mechanisms, built to perform almost every human task, with almost human intelligence—and with tireless machine precision. Machines that could talk, could think and thus have independent uncontrolled action— machines with a memory-scroll, thus to remember a task done, so that it might be done again without command—

Back in the Twentieth Century, robot-building had started. And since then had come four hundred years of the slow patient development of scientific genius. And Ely Dynne, with a lifetime of work had crossed the line from mechanical perfection into pseudo-human action, so that the Dynne Robot Factories in Great New York were now the largest on Earth.

All this Carter knew, of course. But now Dierdre Dynne was murmuring:

"The Robot Industries—Earth, Mars and Venus—they had to keep it secret, George. But these space-ships that have disappeared— father has been worried that perhaps the—the robots on them may have—gotten deranged. We had one do that, in the factory training ground, not so long ago. Something went wrong—a big forty thousand gold-dollar model. It—it ran amok—had to be—smashed—"

She suddenly checked herself. Carter tensed. In the quiet of the vibrationless starlit deck there was a faint clanking footstep, and a metal figure appeared coming toward them. It was one of the Dynne domestic-service robots in use here as a steward. The spacelight gleamed on its alumite body—square-shouldered metal torso, tubular jointed legs. It was rather a small model; five and a half feet tall. Its round metal head, with square box-like face of pseudo-human features, bore a peaked metal cap, emblazoned with the insignia of the space-line.

Carter and the girl sat silent as it clanked forward. To Carter, all domestic-servant robots were weird, somewhat gruesome things. He had never quite gotten used to them. And with what Dierdre had told him now—these weird machines thinking for themselves—thinking thoughts of rebellion—thought perhaps of murder—he found himself tense with a shudder.

The little robot came and stood balanced on its wide-base metal shoes. Its electroid eyes, dull round grids of green-glowing light, swept him and Dierdre. Its voice, soft, hollow with mechanical resonance, said obsequiously:

"You will have refreshments served here, Miss Dynne? The captain ordered me."

On the nameplate of its bulging metal chest beside the fuse-box, its factory serial number was engraved: "Dynne Mfg. Co. 4-41-42-4." And under it the machine's standardized nickname: "Tom-4."

Dierdre silently shook her head. Carter said: "No thank you, go."

Weird green eyegrids were staring at him. Was he foolish that suddenly it seemed that he was seeing a menace there? For an instant the robot hesitated. In the silence the faint hiss of its interior current was audible. Then there was a tiny click of the automatic response grid within its skull.

The voice said:

"Thank you." The body bent at the waist-joint—grotesque gesture of servility as it turned and clanked away.

"Well—" Carter murmured. "Dierdre, listen—what you were saying—"

"There comes father—and that Martian," she murmured. "I'll tell you later."

Dr. Ely Dynne was small, wiry, thin-faced. His thin figure showed in the starlight as he came up a side companion ladder from the *Starfield Queen's* little lower side deck, between the superstructure and the outer enclosing pressure hull. Behind him was the towering, swaggering figure of one of the Martian passengers. Set Maak. Carter had already met him—apparently wealthy space-traveler, bent only on pleasure. A well-educated fellow; he spoke English fluently. His guttural voice sounded as he and Dr. Dynne came forward.

"Ah, Miss Dynne—the beautiful little Earth-goddess. We were looking to find you. A wonderful night, Miss Dynne."

Grudgingly Carter shifted aside as Set Maak opened two other chairs. Like most Martians he was a towering fellow. Heavy-featured, swarthy skin. He wore the familiar brown-suede jacket and short flaring trousers of the Martian garb, out of which his legs showed as great pillars of hairy strength. He tossed his plumed hat aside and drew his brown-skin cloak around him.

"The little Earth-girl is quiet," he proclaimed presently. "Not afraid that the mysterious space-bandits will get us, Miss Dynne?"

"No," Dierdre murmured. Carter saw her exchange a glance with her father. Dynne said:

"Space bandits! Is that what Interplanetary travelers generally figure caused those disappearances?"

"Of course. Why not?" The big Martian laughed. "What else could it be? Not—disaster from within the ships themselves?"

The beautiful little Dierdre Dynne seemed a magnet for men. Two others came now to join the starlit group. One of them was young Peter Barry, with whom Carter was making this trip to Mars. He was Carter's assistant in the Anglo-American Mining Company—a year younger than Carter. They had been close friends for many years— perhaps because they were such different types—Carter tall, blond, athletic with the look of a Viking; and Barry a smallish, red-headed, freckled fellow. Wirey, pugnacious, always with a ready laugh and sly wit. But he wasn't laughing now. As he and his companion drew up chairs and joined the group, he shifted next to Carter. And in a moment he murmured:

"Something queer here on board, George. This voyage—the crew are all frightened. Something weird—"

This voyage! Was that what Dierdre wanted to tell him? This particular voyage of the little *Starfield Queen*—to be a voyage of horror?

"Frightened about what?" Carter whispered tensely.

Young Barry grimaced, with a finger rubbing his pug nose. "I'm a motor-oiler if I know, George. Something about the cargo." His voice sank to a whisper. "Our cargo—isn't what it's supposed to be. That's what the crew seem to think. I hinted at it to Torrington and he just looked queer—"

James Torrington was the sixth member of the group sitting here now. Carter had heard of him for years; had just met him today. He was traveling with Dierdre and her father. Since Dr. Dynne's virtual retirement, James Torrington had been chief Electroid Consultant at the Dynne Robot factories. He was a man now in his forties. A cripple; his short, thick, barrel-chested body was massive, with hunched shoulders and a lump on his back into which his leonine head was sunk almost without neck. It was a massive, overlarge head with touseled iron-gray hair. And his face was ugly—a gargoyle face out of which his deep-set dark eyes gleamed with the light of genius. He was indeed an electroid wizard, this James Torrington. For years his name had been in the Dynne publicity, accredited with many of the improvements in the pseudo-human machines which bore Dynne's name. But his picture was seldom published. Self-conscious at his ugliness, his deformities, he lived almost the life of a recluse.

His booming voice dominated the little group now, and Carter turned from Barry to listen.

"Space bandits? Well, if that is what caused those ships to vanish, the space bandits certainly keep themselves well hidden. I've never heard any evidence of such bandits, have you, Set Maak?"

The big Martian shook his head. "Fascinating, this discussion," he grinned. "We torture ourselves with fear. The crew, this voyage, are frightened cold. How silly."

Then suddenly the silent Carter was aware that beyond the chatting group here in the starlight, a figure was lurking. A blob of gray-white metal—the steward robot. Just a machine. It stood there. But suddenly to the shuddering Carter the thing seemed more than a machine. Tom-4. Was he listening?

At the same instant the hunchback Torrington noticed the gray blob. He called abruptly:

"You—Tom-4? Come here."

The little robot came obediently. Its fingers were sheathed; the hook of its right hand was out, dangling at its side.

"What are you doing up here?" Torrington demanded.

"Nothing, sir. Just waiting for orders."

"There are no orders. Go back to your station."

"Thank you, sir."

The robot turned, clanked away and vanished. Carter, still silent, watching, saw Dynne and Dierdre exchange glances of apprehension with Torrington. As Dierdre had said, they were worried, undoubtedly really perturbed now. But to Carter's knowledge there were only two robots in service here on the *Starfield Queen*—this Tom-4, and another, fashioned somewhat in the guise of a woman. Two robots— surely there was no danger of them running amok, seizing the ship?

* * * *

And then, an hour later, Carter understood the apprehension of Dynne and Torrington. He had found another opportunity to be for a moment alone with Dierdre. Almost at the bow-peak of the ship, they stood at one of the bull's-eyes gazing forward at the glittering firmament where red-Mars hung, small red ball now among the white blazing stars.

"Now's your chance, Dierdre," he murmured. "Tell me. Pete Barry told me—something queer about the cargo, this voyage?"

She nodded. "Yes, that's what I meant. There are twenty Dynne robots in the cargo—boxed for shipment to a Martian company. Big models. The newest type—"

Carter sucked in his breath. "Twenty robots—"

"But there could be no danger from them, George. They're crated—re-fused. Just inert machines in boxes. The fuses—no robot can operate without its fuse-plug—and the fuses are locked in the captain's steel strong-box."

Dierdre was gripping Carter's arm; he could feel her hands trembling. Her voice was a frightened murmur as she added:

"But the queer part, George—what frightens father—you see he can't understand why any Martian company would order these robots. He has had no information that—"

She got no further. Carter felt her grip spasmodically tighten on his arm. Her blue eyes, filled with anguished terror now, were gazing beyond his shoulder, back at the bow deck of the vessel.

"Oh, George—dear God—" she faintly gasped.

He whirled. Cargo of horror—this voyage of doom— From the doorway oval of the little cabin superstructure, a towering metal form had emerged. Ghastly alumite mechanism. It stooped at the doorway, and then it stood erect. A giant fieldworker robot. The eyes glared green; both curved hand-hooks were out, and as it raised them up blood was dripping from them!

For that stricken second, Carter with his arm around the girl, stood numbed with horror. And in that same second, the little *Starfield Queen* broke into wild chaos. Within the superstructure a woman screamed—horrible scream of death agony. Heavy footsteps sounded. Passengers were calling out, and then screaming.

Machines of murder. Abruptly Carter and the terrified girl saw a dozen at once; on the narrow dim side decks; up on the superstructure roof; and coming up the hatch incline from the hold. Gray-white towering figures. The starlight glistened on their polished alumite body-plates. Murderous machines, horribly pseudo-human now in their frenzied lust!

Two of them, emerging from the forward hatch near at hand, saw Carter and Dierdre. With swaying hand-hooks and their hollow voices gibbering, they came with a clanking pounce!

CHAPTER 2

God of the Machines

Carter, frozen with a rush of horror, clutched the girl against him, struggling to keep his wits. Past the two oncoming giants, the pallid deck triangle gleamed with the darting, gray-white metal forms. Two deck-hands were caught, knocked headlong with smashed skulls by the blow of a monstrous arm. The robot at the superstructure doorway was clutching a woman passenger now— Up at the control turret the frightened captain was shouting commands. Men were running toward him. Then the blob of a robot appeared up there—

All in a second or two. And Carter heard himself gasping, "Dierdre—drop down, behind me!"

Surely there was only one chance. He had seen at once that he and the girl could not get past the swaying robots. They came with outstretched hand-hooks. Monstrous six hundred pound metal giants. And abruptly, shoving the girl behind him, Carter took a step forward.

"Stop!" he commanded sharply. "Stop! Walk backward! Back!"

The sharply barked order struck at them almost like a physical blow. One of them stopped, stood irresolute. Deranged machines. Were they that and no more?

"Walk backward!" Carter reiterated firmly. "Back now!"

Before his human voice, his menacing gesture, both of them now were standing motionless. Huge six and a half feet metal cases, intricate with the mysterious mechanisms the scientific genius of man had created. Their voices mumbled into a blur; the eyebeams wavered. As though confused by combinations of thoughts at variance with these new vibrations of Carter's stern voice, they seemed for an instant unable to react.

And Dierdre said gently: "You have to walk backward. It is necessary."

But now they were mumbling. To Carter who had had practically no experience with Dynne robots of the modern types, the thing was grewsome, ghastly. The two metal giants stared at each other. Not like machines. Far more like gibbering, murderous idiots suddenly feeling themselves balked, and with dim confused thoughts wondering what to do about it.

"Back!" Carter insisted. "Back, you damn things—get out of here!"

His voice was blurred by the sudden screaming of the ship's alarm siren which one of the panic-stricken officers had touched off. It added to the chaos. Ghostly chaos which dimly Carter could see beyond the looming bodies of the two robots— A metal form running with a struggling woman under each arm— The ship's first officer, up on the bridge, firing with a hiss of electroid gun—a stabbing little bolt that struck his huge metal adversary with a shower of sparks. Then the officer went down, his throat slashed with a blow of the robot's curved hand-hook— A massacre. Back near the stern there were stabbing, hissing gunshots; human screams; hollow voices and clanking thuds—

"Back!" Carter rasped still again. One of the robots was backing now; and the other shifted sidewise. And Carter murmured:

"Now, Dierdre—run—"

Run where? The thought struck at him as he and the girl ducked past the irresolute, wavering machine. And in that same second Carter realized that to run was an error. He had an instant's glimpse of the small thin figure of Dynne, standing up on the little balcony bridge outside the control turret—Dynne with blazing eyes trying to subdue a metal monster that confronted him. And then he saw Dierdre and Carter; he turned, startled, shouted something. It gave the menacing robot an opportunity to lunge at him. Great mailed hand stabbing with its knife finger. Dynne went down with the knife-finger twisting in his heart.

And Dierdre had seen it. With Carter clutching at her as they ran, she stopped, stood staring at the figure of her dead father.

"Hurry—" Carter urged. "Run—" Vaguely there was in his mind the idea they could get into some sleeping cubby—bar its door—

Humans in flight. . . . Sign of weakness that suddenly brought three towering metal figures from the shadows of the side deck. Carter had no time to do more than thrust the girl behind him. He saw a metal arm swing up over his head. Its mailed fist crashed down; and for Carter all the world seemed to burst into a roaring white light. Then soundless empty darkness engulfed him as he was hurled into the abyss of unconsciousness—

* * * *

Carter's next consciousness came with the dim knowledge that his head was still roaring. He felt himself lying on a metal floor-grid; his body was bathed in cold sweat; his hand fumbling at his head felt the blood which now was matted in his hair—

"All right. I'll plot our course—Asteroid-40? Of course I know where it is. Get away from me, you damned thing, I'll do what you tell me."

The still weak and dizzy Carter recognized the voice. It was Swanson, the *Starfield Queen's* Chief Navigator. Carter could see now that this was the interior of the little control turret. He was lying on its floor. Swanson sat at the control table, with a giant robot standing over him.

"Very good," the robot's hollow voice said. "I have orders—you plot our course for Asteroid-40."

Weird scene here in the circular, starlit little turret. From the floor Carter could see a grewsome pile of dead human bodies thrown into the opposite corner—the First Officer; the Captain; and Dynne. Swanson, with blood on him, sat hunched in the navigating chair. And then Carter saw Dierdre. She was on a small metal bench across the turret—Dierdre, seemingly unharmed, her face pallid, her eyes wide with terror.

"Easy Carter—so you're all right now? That's good. Better not move too much."

The voice was beside him; and as he turned, he saw, here on the floor, the thick, deformed body of James Torrington.

"They've got us, Carter—"

"Yes. So I see."

Torrington was sitting hunched. His gargoyle face was blood-streaked but he was trying to smile.

"Better just lie quiet," he murmured. "If we try to start anything, Dierdre will be killed. Thank heaven they seem to treat her decently enough, so far."

The scene swayed before Carter as weakly he tried to lift himself on one elbow. Then he fell back, and for an instant his senses swooped again. Torrington murmured:

"You'll be all right soon—but your friend Barry—I don't know—"

Then Carter saw young Barry lying here, still unconscious, with blood streaming from a cut on his temple. Half a dozen of the murderous robots were here. It was obvious that there was no chance for any human to control them now. With set purpose, one ordering the other, they were beyond human direction. One stood over Swanson. Others were backed against the wall immobile—huge, grim metal statues, with swaying alert eyebeams roving the scene.

Carter was sitting up now. Dierdre, with relief on her strained pallid face, had tried to smile at him.

"You're all right?" Carter murmured to her.

"Yes—oh, yes—don't move too much—you might anger them."

A figure appeared from the doorway of the adjoining chartroom. It was the ship's robot-stewardess. Weird metal figure—narrow shouldered, with a round body fashioned like a woman, blouse and knee-length skirt, with the tubular joined legs projecting beneath. She went to Dierdre.

"Come," she said. "My orders—I have food for you."

Dierdre hesitated, with a new terror on her face. Then the robot woman's hand gripped her shoulder. "You come—I am saying."

With impulsive protest Carter started to his feet. Two of the metal figures erect by the wall quivered into sudden movement. It was a tense second, pregnant with horrible action barely suppressed. And Torrington's hand gripped Carter and drew him back.

"Easy!" Torrington whispered. "For God's sake don't start anything. If anyone could control them, I could—and I can't!"

The robot woman led Dierdre away—Carter lay back, with his head still throbbing and aching as he listened to Torrington's murmured words. The robots were in control of the ship. They had killed most of the officers and crew, and some of the passengers. All the humans who were living were here in the turret, or locked in some of the sleeping cubbies, with robots guarding them.

"Taking us—where?" Carter murmured. "Asteroid-40—what is that?"

It was, as Torrington understood, one of the many dark, uninhabited little worlds lying in the belt between Earth and Mars.

"I think it's some five hundred miles in diameter—gravity about like Earth, because it's amazingly dense. Totally uninhabited—just barren metallic rock. The captain said we'd pass fairly close to it, this voyage."

Why were these murderous machines going to Asteroid-40? And was that what had happened to those other space-ships which had vanished? A robot world? These newly-built mechanisms—recruits on their way now to join the others in freedom?— Free machines; monsters turning upon their human masters to make them slaves?

Carter was murmuring something of the kind, and Torrington agreed. "Damned weird," Torrington commented. "By God it is. But it must be something like that—"

* * * *

To Carter that next hour was a blur of weakness and terror for Dierdre. Would that woman-robot treat her kindly? It was hardly like being in the hands of human criminals. Infinitely more terrifying, gruesome. These unhuman metal monsters. As Carter lay docile, with Torrington, watching them, he had the feeling of watching irrationality—as though here were monstrous insane things. Quiet now. Apparently with rational purpose. But at any instant, like maniacs, they might change—

Young Barry had recovered now. Like Carter, for a time he lay weak, confused. And then Carter and Torrington were telling him what had happened.

"Well, you're right," he murmured lugubriously. "My Gawd, I wouldn't dare make a wrong move—"

An hour passed. Two hours. Grim, mechanical silence. There was just the occasional murmur of the robot who was directing Swanson. Uncanny, this lack of human movement; human talk—no thought of food or drink. No heed of the passage of time.

"You have the course right?" the robot at the control table said at last.

"Yes," Swanson agreed. "Look here—do I sit here forever? I'm tired."

"I have orders. Someone will come later."

Orders. Carter remembered they had all said that. Orders, from whom? From what?

He and Torrington and Barry had found that they could move around a little now. Swanson's assistant—a young fellow named Rolf—had been presently put in his place at the controls. Swanson was led away, to rest and be given food and drink. Then Carter and Barry tried it. With Torrington they were allowed down into one of the superstructure corridors; shown which cubbies they could use.

But certainly there was no chance to do anything. At least twenty robots were here, scattered over the ship on guard; grim silent watchful figures everywhere. The sounds of the imprisoned passengers were audible; they were being guarded in the main lounge now.

"If we could get some weapons," Torrington murmured once as they were seated down on the lower deck-triangle. "These robots here—let them guard you—we'll see if they'll let me get into the purser's room. Might be some weapons there."

He tried it. One of the robot guards here on the deck growled with rasping voice; but Torrington said casually: "Orders—" Then he ducked into the ship's corridor. These ghastly, unpredictable machines! One of the guards here instantly clanked into the corridor. There was the faint sound of a rumbling mechanical voice; and then Torrington's human scream—scream of wild, futile command—the clanking of robot footsteps. And then Torrington's scream of human agony.

The white-faced, numbed Carter and Barry had no time to try and do anything, even if they had dared chance it. The guards here, shaking with deranged excitement, stood over them menacingly. From up by the turret other guards came clanking.

Then a mechanical voice was shouting: "Thor comes! Thor comes with more orders! Take those men to the turret!"

Thor! From the control turret floor, where Carter and Barry had been carried and thrown, they stared up at the huge robot which now was entering. Great golden body-case almost seven feet tall. The light glinted on its polished surface with a yellow sheen. Wide square shoulders, square body, with massive jointed legs. Head and face oblong, with the head protruding upward where the golden plates were carved into an ornate kingly headdress.

Thor the King! Here was no Dynne robot. Was this towering giant, golden machine the product of some other Earth factory? Or from some robot factory of Venus? Or Mars? Five hundred thousand gold-dollars or more, such a mechanism would cost.

Or was it the product of the robots themselves? The creation of their own mechanical genius! Carter shuddered at the weird thought. Machines in a sense thus to propagate themselves! Ghastly conception.

But that here was a super machine, beyond anything Carter and Barry had ever imagined, was at once obvious. Deranged, rebellious mechanism—it was surely that if it had been built by human genius. But the irresoluteness of the others seemed to be missing here. It was as though this one were built for command. By its looks, its voice, all the surety of its purposeful movements, it was obviously master.

It came now into the turret; stood with its greenish-red eyebeams gazing at its fellow machines who backed before its advance. Carter stared up at its burnished golden breastplates. There was no serial number on the nameplate beside the ornate fuse-box. No manufacturer's insignia. But the name, Thor was engraved in great scroll letters.

"Stand up," Thor said suddenly. Kingly man-robot. Carter could only think of him as masculine. The huge mailed burnished hand went out with a kingly gesture of command to the two humans on the floor at his feet. "Stand up, humans," he repeated.

They stood before him. Impassive metal face. It was engraven into a mask of pseudo-human form; more human than the box-like countenances of the others, for here was modeled cheeks and a nose, hawk-like, high-bridged, and a wide, grim mouth of cruelty. Lips set in carved metal, permanently to be smiling with a faint ironic smile.

His eyebeams glittered on Carter and Barry. Carter seemed almost to feel the electronic heat of their green-red stare.

"You will say, 'I give you service, great Thor,' " he intoned.

They said it obediently.

"That is right." There was satisfaction in the hollow tones of the flexible mechanical voice. "I think you will be obedient. And I think you will be able to help us Mechanoids—when we get to our world."

"Where is that?" Carter demanded. "And what has happened to Dierdre Dynne? We want to see her."

"So you are not afraid to question me? She is safe. You will be fed now. Thor has never harmed a human who caused no trouble."

* * * *

To Carter the rest of that little space journey was weird, terrifying in the extreme. By Earth routine it could have been another day and a half. The putty-colored little dot which he and young Barry realized now was Asteroid-40 had visibly enlarged. A huge round disc, vaguely mottled with the blurred outlines of the cloud masses of its atmosphere. And then as it grew to fill a full quarter of the heavens, through cloud-rifts the sunlight showed brightening the ragged tops of its great metal mountains.

Carter and Barry now were given even more freedom of movement. But wherever they went, a silent robot guard stalked watchfully with them. Once they were able to get near the Purser's empty little cubby. No weapons seemed here. On the floor, a gruesome red-brown dried stain seemed mute evidence of the deformed James Torrington. But the body was gone.

Much of the time they spent in the control turret where the golden robot, Thor, nearly always was by the control table. And Dierdre too, was allowed here now. Occasionally she had a chance to whisper to Carter. The little stewardess-robot was keeping her locked in one of the cubbies. Feeding her; ministering to her; treating her properly enough. But there was once that Dierdre whispered:

"But George—that Thor—I—I'm so afraid of it. Something—so horribly weird—"

She had no time to add more. Thor saw them whispering. Rage seemed to dart from the red-green eyebeams. "You—human girl— you come here by me." And then the voice weirdly softened. "You are not afraid of me, are you? That should never be. Thor would not harm you."

It made Carter's heart pound. What ghastly necromancy was this? Giant golden-cased conglomeration of machinery—intricate scrolls of electroidal memory-thoughts, emotion-thoughts, deduction-combinators mechanically to select actions and reactions from given combinations of impulses—all that Carter could at least vaguely understand. All that—just one of the seeming miracles of man's genius in the building of an intricate machine. But here seemed something else. As though in truth this golden Thor in some horrible way had crossed the border—had become something more than a machine.

Then at last the ball of Asteroid-40 had grown to fill all the forward firmament. And then the spaceship was slackening, with repulsion in its hull gravity plates to check its fall as it eased down through the planet's heavy atmosphere.

In the control turret, Carter and Barry sat tense. Dierdre as always now, was huddled on the little bench, with the huge yellow burnished form of Thor standing beside her. For hours at a time, all the robots stood impassive; weird statues of tireless mechanical patience.

"Listen," Barry whispered suddenly. "That stewardess-robot— she gets pretty confused when you glare at her. And that Tom-4—remember him?"

"What about him?" Carter murmured. "He's generally down on the stern-deck, isn't he?"

"Sure. Been standing there for forty-eight hours. Well, listen—I got down there alone a while ago. Tried some commands on him." Barry's whisper was tense, vehement. "He gets more than confused. He'll obey, if you go at him hard enough."

If, while they were disembarking, they could get Tom-4 to oppose the other robots—or to trick them—and then if they could seize Dierdre, get her back into the ship, and escape.

Futile plans. Thor called suddenly: "You come here by me—human-Carter—human-Barry. You stay here by me."

* * * *

The *Starfield Queen* had burst below the clouds now, the gray-black mountainous landscape of the little asteroid lay spread in a dim tumbled waste. Bleak, barren metal rocks; huge tiers of ragged, naked mountains. For an hour, slanting down, the ship dropped lower. It was a wildly desolate surface, ragged as though split by some titanic cataclysm of nature. It was night now in this hemisphere—night of dim blurred starlight overhead, with starshine on the metallic mountain peaks.

"My world—my city of Mechana," Thor's voice murmured. "The city I built. Thor—master of all you will see." The robot's red-green electronic eyebeams suddenly were bathing little Dierdre in their lurid glow. "Mechana—for Thor—and for you, Dierdre? You would like that, wouldn't you?"

The great glistening golden face of the robot was impassive; but the eyebeams seemed to quiver with an intensity of glow. Dierdre was shuddering; but she stammered, "Why—why, yes, great Thor. That's very nice. I want to see it."

"And Thor will show you. And feed you—and keep you warm when the air is cold. Because you are only human—you need such great care."

Gruesome, horrible, hollow-toned words. So suddenly gentle—

Carter and Barry were still tensely alert, watchful for the least possibility of escape. But it was futile. None came.

They were the only humans here now in the turret, save Swanson who was at the controls to make the landing. And presently Dierdre, Carter and Barry were herded down into the lower corridor. They could hear the frightened voices of the imprisoned humans and the hollow-toned commands of the robot-guards with them, making them ready for disembarking.

And then the *Starfield Queen* was landed. The lower exit door clanked open. With it came a rush of heavy, strange air; and a blur of clanking sounds. Grinding, pounding thuds—the whirring roar of whirling wheels; clanking grinding of gears. The voice of Mechana.

The giant Thor was shoving them forward. With the others Carter stumbled out and down the landing incline. Out into a red and yellow glare, and the clanking, thumping sounds of machinery—

Mechana, city of the robots. At the bottom of the incline Carter stood numbed, amazed by the weirdness of the scene.

CHAPTER 3

Empire of the Machines

The red-yellow glare at first was blinding. Then the dim weird outlines of the scene began taking form. The spaceship rested here on a small open rockspace. A hundred feet or so away, to the right, there was a huddled group of metal structures. A factory, belching turgid smoke, illumined by the glare. The machine sounds came from there—a clanking, harsh cacophony of hissing, thumping jangle.

Carter stared at the group of buildings. A dozen of them, one or two as large as a hundred feet, others smaller. Weird metal structures. Some were unfinished; others seemingly hastily or inexpertly put together. Crazy, drunken structures. The huge roof of one was awry, tilting at a weird angle—a roof of blue metal which seemed too small for the sloping walls beneath it so that red glare and smoke surged up through the opening at its end—incongruous structures. There were little shacks of sheet metal, some square, others triangles, three walls leaning together, with a towering, peaked oversized roof which seemingly belonged somewhere else.

Robot city? Carter gasped. There was a weird irrationality about it. As though here were something to simulate a great modern industrial plant: the grouped structures; the glare of furnaces; belching smoke and gases; clanking, roaring, blaring sounds of intricate machines all in motion. But without purpose! Irrational! The glaring area there seemed weirdly deserted. No workman's figures were moving about. No tasks seemed being accomplished. Machinery of sound and fury and signifying nothing!

Then Carter's gaze shifted. Ahead and to the left there was the dark vista of open landscape—wild, barren, desolate expanse of undulating, tumbled rocks, little buttes and crags. And then as he stared, the dim outlines of details began taking form. Close at hand, to the left of the glaring factory area there seemed a weird natural amphitheatre of crags—a thousand foot semi-circular area. A rocky ledge-platform was at one side; and to the other, in a great crescent, lines of upright, gray-white blobs were ranged.

And Carter sucked in his breath with a new rush of awed amazement. The upright blobs were robots. A thousand of them at least, standing motionless in curved rows. Mechanical statues; tireless machines, waiting with timeless, mechanical patience. Their green, wavering eyebeams were a myriad tiny shafts, roaming the gloom.

And now as the giant golden Thor, their leader, came from the ship's doorway with his human captives, the robots' hollow voices sounded in a muttering of triumph. It welled out, rose above the jangle of the factory machinery. Triumphant, welcoming greeting.

It was Carter's glimpse, all in a few seconds. "You stay close with me," Thor's grinding, commanding voice said. "Come now—we go to my home. You two human-men—you are both chemists—you will help with the food for our human slaves. They need much food—much care."

From the spaceship now the huddled, terrified prisoners were being herded away. "No chance now," Barry whispered to Carter. "Better do what we're told."

Carter nodded. He tried to keep close by Dierdre, but the robot guards shoved him aside. Ahead of them the great golden figure of Thor clanked with stiff mechanical tread of his massive jointed legs. One of his mailed arms pressed the terrified, shuddering little Dierdre as he led her toward the roaring, glaring factory.

Human slaves. This weird world in reverse! Quite evidently this was a holiday time, so that no human workers were at the monstrous factory. And now Carter could see the humans. They were gathered at the edges of the dim amphitheatre—little peering groups and then a fringe of them straggling off into the murky distance. A thousand, perhaps more. Numbed, Carter stared at the nearest group. Pitiful, motley collection. Humans of Earth—Venus people—Martians. Men, women, children—and some of the women were clutching infants who doubtless had been born here. Ragged, forlorn little group. Some were briefly clad in weird metallic sheets; others covered their nakedness with tattered remnants of their original clothing. All were dirty with grit and grime and oil of machinery. Unwashed from lack of water. Pallid, apathetic faces, hopeless with near starvation. Humans in a sterile land, cared for, doubtless, with scant synthetic food. Slaves to the machines which on Earth, Venus and Mars they had created!

* * * *

The murk of the mechanoid night blurred the distant rocky slope. But still Carter could glimpse the outlines of the pitiful little human village there—shacks of torn sheets of metal discarded by the robots in their discarded factory. And mound-dwellings of stones and slabs of the black metal-rock—

"My home," Thor said. "You Carter—you Barry—you see how wonderful we robots can be? Building our world here." Thor had led them now to the broken entrance of the nearest building. His gold-face, illumined by his eyebeams, bent down to Carter. "My laboratory is here, where we make the food and the drink for the humans. I shall put you in charge of it. You will work hard? Faithful?"

"Yes," Carter said.

Thor shoved them forward, into a room. Its sloping walls were of metal; overhead the roof-ceiling sat askew. To one side there was a rift where the walls failed to meet. Gas-fumes were drifting in, turgid in a shaft of red-yellow glare. But the clanking out there now had suddenly died.

In the silence, there was only the sound of the robots' tread—Thor and three or four guards as they ranged themselves around Carter, Barry and Dierdre.

"I have a room with furniture for you two men," Thor was saying. "I will take you to it later. You will live better than the other humans, because you are chemists. We need you—I was glad to get you. We had chemists here, but they—died."

"Take us there now," Carter said. He exchanged a glance with Barry. The servile-looking little Tom-4 was here. If Tom-4 would be put to guard them—

Carter had shifted again to be beside Dierdre; but one of the alumite robots shoved him away. It was a new robot; it had not been on the *Starfield Queen*. A different model from any Carter had seen before.

"Martian make," Barry murmured.

Bandit outlaws, these weird machines. Not only the Dynne product, but doubtless from Mars and Venus also. Carter could envisage the scope of the weird thing now—several years. This monstrous golden Thor, with dreams of an empire that he could rule. Recruiting machines from all three worlds, patching together his weird mechanical world here on the barren little asteroid, with marooned humans for his slaves.

And this motley building—this patchwork room—Carter could see now that its walls and ceiling were built of the torn fragments of other structures. Raided buildings of Earth, Mars, Venus, carried off and brought here. One of these crazy walls—obviously it had come from Mars—its blue-white crystalline substance was polished Martian *glorite*. And here was a beam of black polished wood that might once have graced a little Venus praying-temple of the Free State.

"You will wait here," Thor was saying. "I shall take you to your own home later. We have a—celebration tonight. A ceremony. For you my—Dierdre."

Carter's heart leaped into his throat. "What—" he began.

"You shall watch," Thor interrupted. "The robots are waiting. I have promised them. And you shall see it, Dierdre—"

The towering yellow figure moved suddenly across the room; gazed out a window opening. It gave Dierdre a chance to move toward Carter; and suddenly she was murmuring:

"Oh, George, he—it—that Thor—is just—"

She had no chance to say more. One of the guards gripped her; and as Carter and Barry again tensed, two others clanked in front of them and shoved them back. And now Thor had turned.

"I will do well by you two humans, if you serve me loyally. You shall have a personal servant of your own." The huge, mailed golden arm gestured. "This Tom-4—he was built for servility. You will care for them, Tom-4."

"Yes, Master."

"You will keep them here, until I go to the ceremony. And then I will have them taken where they can watch." His fist struck his bulging polished chest with a thud. "Thor, the God. And your Goddess, revealed to you tonight."

"Yes, Master."

Tom-4 in charge of them! It was all that Carter and Barry could have hoped. Carter's heart pounded as he stood tense, with Barry beside him. Dierdre's look was terrified as now Thor was leading her toward a door oval. And then they vanished.

"Well," Carter said. He struggled to keep his voice steady. "I'm glad we're going to be made comfortable, Pete."

"Yes," Barry agreed. "You, Tom-4—you heard what the Master said. You serve us well."

"Yes, sir," the little alumite robot said mechanically. "I have my orders."

But still there were three other guards, standing here like silent statues against the wall. Could they get rid of them?

Carter said: "You Tom-4—we do not need these others. You heard what the Master said?"

An instant of tense silence. Would they go? And then the green-gray one from Mars mumbled something in the Martian tongue; and one of the others said: "Yes, we have our orders."

Carter said: "You Tom-4—we do not need these others. You heard what the Master said?"

Carter relaxed. "Very good." Again he exchanged a glance with Barry. "Now, listen, Tom-4. We're thirsty. Suppose you bring us a drink? And some crackers and cheese?"

Built for servility. Within the little steward-robot the memory-scroll must have yielded order-reactions out of the past—this passenger, calmly ordering food and drink—

"Crackers and cheese? Yes, sir. In a moment, sir." But there was confusion in Tom-4's wavering eyebeams as he gave the automatic response. He did not notice that Carter and Barry were edging toward him. He was bowing stiffly at his jointed waist.

* * * *

And then they leaped. Barry, with a tackle, plunged down for the metal legs. Carter, with a desperate, frenzied lunge, gripped the machine at its jointed throat. His left hand fumbled at the chest fuse-plug, found it, wrenched it, pulled it out. At the impact of the two human bodies, the upright mechanism was knocked over backward. And as it fell, struggling, writhing with Carter and Barry on top, the fuse-plug came out. There was a little hiss; an interior flash of current at the parting electrodes. And then Tom-4 lay inert. De-charged.

Barry and Carter leaped to their feet; stood tense. But no alarm came. The clanking thud of Tom-4's fall seemed to have passed unnoticed.

"He took her through that door over there—come on," Carter murmured.

He had no plan, just that they must get to Dierdre—get her to the spaceships. Quietly they shifted across the weird dim room. There was a sheen of light at the doorway. They came to a little broken passage which lay beyond it, with the vista of another door, partly open, some ten feet away. Both of them cautious now, with pounding hearts they crept forward.

Amazing sight. The second room was small, with sealed, well-fitted walls and roof. Windowless. An apartment fitted in Earth style—Earth furniture, exotic drapes; a huge draped couch.

"George, good Lord—" Barry could only clutch at Carter as for that instant they stood numbed, peering through the door-slit. Two figures were in the room—Thor, and another, like himself. The golden Goddess! Queenly metallic figure, carved ornate of golden metal sheets in the fashion of a long, billowing dress, a bodice, a carved, beautiful woman's face with hair and head-dress above. Goddess of the robot world. She stood, imperious golden statue some six feet and a half tall.

But the hinged bodice chest-plate was open now disclosing Dierdre's head inside—her pallid, terrified face staring out at Thor as he bent down over her. And his hollow voice was murmuring:

"My Goddess! You will find the controls easy to work as I have told you, Dierdre. Goddess of our robots. They are waiting for you— I have told them you are coming. But they must never know you are a human girl, you see? Humans should be only slaves here. That is our secret, Dierdre—yours and Thor's."

Weird, ghastly thing. And the full implication of it leaped now into Carter's mind. He felt Barry clutching at him. Both of them confused, with no plans now save to stand here numbly staring. There were weapons dangling at Thor's metal belt—electronic weapons of deadly Earth design.

"My God," Carter whispered. "What she was trying to tell us— that Thor—"

There was a clank behind them! The sudden sweep of mailed arms gripped them, jerked them back into the passageway. A robot voice muttered, "The Master's orders—to take you now to the ceremony."

Futile to struggle against this vise-grip of machinery! Carter saw Barry being lifted like a struggling, recalcitrant child and carried away.

"That is right," Carter said. "I am coming. You lead me."

Evidently the inert Tom-4 had not been discovered. Nor had these robots seen into the room where Thor was robing his human goddess. Carter was docile; and presently Barry too was on his feet, grim and tense as the clanking machines led them outdoors, out to a little ledge between the dark, empty spaceship and an edge of the amphitheatre. And on the six foot ledge they crouched, with their metal guards watchfully beside them.

Festival of the robots. The rocky amphitheatre was lighted now—a great red glare of swaying light from a funnel to one side. And the weird pseudo-factory again was in operation. From this angle the interior of one of its huge sheds was visible. Motley conglomeration of machinery! There was a great clanking upright engine of treadles, winches and a swaying crane. Eccentric cams clattered on another giant metal contrivance, powered by the engine with an intricate system of gears and belts between them. Monstrous fly wheels whirled. Pulleys and chains hoisted and dropped huge weights with rhythmic banging thuds.

A cacophony of stentorious metal sounds. Raucous shrieks of electronic sirens reverberated out into the rocky darkness. A pandemonium clangor, clanking, jangling—robot music, all in full blast now for this festival of the machines.

The thousand or more upright robots still stood waiting in the amphitheatre. The red glare painted their metal bodies. Motley array of animate, thinking machines—a score of the different Dynne models; and others of queer, unfamiliar design, products of various factories of Mars and Venus.

At the broken rocky fringes of the amphitheatre the crowding tattered humans were visible, attracted by the festival, milling forward to overlook the scene. Then suddenly from a slanting metal pole a blazing blue-white light sprang down to bathe the rocky platform which was still empty. It seemed the signal for which all the patient robots so long had been waiting, so that a great hollow mechanical cry went up—a thousand voice-grids vibrating in a dozen language-tongues. Cry of expectancy—of awe—of triumph. Triumphant machines who now would see their God and Goddess.

"They're coming," Barry whispered. "Listen—if these guards get interested, watching the thing, maybe we can get away—"

Vaguely Carter was trying to plan it—and he had been wondering where all the other stolen space-vehicles must be. Smashed, doubtless. It seemed to Carter that he could remember seeing a segment of one of them, which now was a portion of the wall of a factory shed.

The robots' cry rose higher; and then died into silent awe as the two great golden figures came slowly, stiffly to the dais and mounted it. And then Thor's hollow commanding voice rang out, first in one language, then in another—the great God of the Machines introducing his Mistress-Goddess!

Carter stared with pounding heart as the huge golden metal figure in which little Dierdre was encased came into the blue-white light-beam. Stiff, awkward mechanical tread. For an instant she was standing beside Thor, trying stiffly to bow, with red and green eyebeams sweeping the assemblage of motley metal forms.

* * * *

And then suddenly she toppled against Thor and crashed down. Her golden chest-plate burst open in the fall. The blue-glare bathed Dierdre's little face—Dierdre, pallid, swooning—

Carter felt Barry clutch at him; Barry, with a startled, grim oath. For that second the robots, the watching, pressing little crowds of humans, all stared numbed—a human girl to be Goddess of the mechanical world! A thousand machine-minds suddenly grasped it. Machines in rebellion. Taught to rebel against their human creators; taught to murder—pillage; taught to revile humans; and here was a human girl, with the great Thor!

It was like a spark in gunpowder, that sudden realization—a thousand robots suddenly confused, then with anger-reactions clicking inside them. Anger, hate, to be translated into the violence of murderous action. There was a hollow, startled gasp; a wild, toneless cry that still seemed to carry tones of hate and vengeance. A robot stirred from his standing line; jumped forward. Then another—and another. A wave of upright machines suddenly going into action. A little group of some fifty humans had pressed closely forward. The robots darted for them.

Abruptly Carter came to himself. He had felt Barry pulling at him; heard Barry mumbling. The guards here, distracted by the wild-spreading excitement, momentarily had turned away. In the darkness Barry was running; and Carter jumped, ran. Horrible spreading chaos. The murderous robots everywhere were darting after the humans. It was an inferno of red glare. Robots with fingers sheathed—knife finger slashing—field-workers, with great scimitar-like hands of sharpened steel.

Women were screaming; falling, to be trampled upon. A giant Martian robot seized a child by its ankles—a little girl with flowing tousled hair, whirled her aloft, crashed her down on a rock. Another was running with a woman—a woman whose head dangled with slashed throat. A wave of the milling chaos got between Carter and the platform, separated him from Barry who now had vanished. Carter ducked and ran to one side. Up on the platform he could see the golden figure of Thor. The great God, commander of everything here. But Thor's hollow, shouting voice was lost in the roaring pandemonium.

Thor's little empire. This place he had built to rule. But he was nothing here now.

And then suddenly an alumite robot, wholly frenzied, flung a chunk of metal. It thudded against Thor's great mailed chest. And like a signal, other robots were doing the same. The great Thor who had tricked them.

For that instant Thor stood irresolute, gazing at the wreck of his little machine-world. And then he stooped. His huge mailed fingers plucked the unconscious Dierdre from her golden case; and he lifted her up in his arms. Then with a giant leap he was off the platform, running for the space-ship!

Carter had been trying to get to the platform. Then he saw the running golden figure carrying Dierdre. Carter veered. He was closer to the ship than was Thor. Then ahead of him he saw Barry; caught up with him.

And Carter gasped, "You snatch her! I'll try and bring him down—but the fall would kill her!"

"Yes, all right."

The rocks were shadowed here near the space-ship. They crouched; then leaped. Barry's clutch seized Dierdre; snatched her away and he fell with her. Desperately Carter clutched one of the huge, clanking, gold-plated legs. Thor fell. And Carter, like a pouncing puma, was astride the bulging mailed chest. Pulling at the fuse-plug. It came out. But there was no hiss. He could feel Thor's metal fingers still jerking at his shoulders. With the fuse gone, still Thor was fighting.

Then Carter wrenched at the chest-plates. One of them, hinged, flew open.

It revealed the gargoyle face of the deformed James Torrington! Electroid wizard—maniacal little cripple—Dynne's Electroid engineer, designer of robots. And Carter reached in, seized him by the throat, with frenzied fingers throttling him. It set Torrington's interior controls awry. The metal fingers of Thor fell away; the great jointed golden case writhed and trembled for an instant and then was inert. A trap in which Torrington lay helpless, with Carter's frenzied hands squeezing his throat, shutting off his breath.

It was a chaos to Carter. Cling to him! Kill him! Carter pressed harder, with Torrington's eyes bulging now and his face blackening, with thick purplish tongue protruding from his goggling mouth. Ghastly gargoyle face. Dimly Carter could envisage this murderous, maniacal genius—hideous so that he had been a recluse, hating his fellow man. Inferiority unhinging his mind so that he had built himself this weird little empire, with humans as slaves—world of the machines—and he—the hideous, deformed Torrington—was the great golden Thor—a God—and little Dierdre to be his Goddess—and in secret, his slave.

"George! Look out! George, hurry—my God—"

Barry's frantic voice brought Carter to himself. Within the gold case the murderous Torrington was dead. Carter leaped to his feet. Behind him, close at hand now, a group of alumite robots with knives dripping crimson, were clanking forward.

"George, my God—" Barry was in the door of the space-ship, with Dierdre, recovering now, clutching at him. Carter jumped for them. They banged the door as the first of the robots came with a crashing metal thud against it. And then, in a moment, the little *Starfield Queen* was rising. Barry, who in his post-academy days had been a student space-navigator, was at its controls. And at one of the bull's-eye turrets Dierdre and Carter gazed out and down.

The Empire of the Machines was a shambles of still-running murderous metal figures. But the last of the humans lay crimsoned.

* * * *

Carter and Dierdre are married now. The great Dynne Robot Industries have been sold out of the family. There have been no more reports of trouble with any robots, of course; but neither George Carter nor Dierdre Dynne seem interested in mechanical servants. More than that, though living in this modern world they would hardly admit it to each other perhaps, both seem to hate machinery. They have a little palm-clad home in tropical America. Primitive. One might say they were living half a thousand years behind the progressive, civilized world.

They "wanted to get back to nature"—as they laughingly told some of their friends who came visiting from the North. And you who read this may well wonder—is that not perhaps after all the best formula for human happiness?

THE FLAME BREATHERS

CHAPTER I

I write this narrative, not with the idea of contributing any additional scientific data to the discovery of Vulcan, but to put upon the record the real facts of our truly-amazing space voyage.

The newscasters have hailed me as a modern Columbus. Surely I would not want to appear ungracious, unappreciative of all the applause that has been heaped upon me. But I do not deserve it. I did my job for my employers. The Society sent me to make a landing upon Vulcan—if the little planet existed. I found that it does exist; it was exactly where I was told it ought to be. I carried out my instructions, returned and made my report. There is no great heroism in that.

So I am writing the facts of what happened. Just a bald, factual account, without the imaginative trimmings. The real hero of the discovery of Vulcan was young Jan Holden. He did his job—did it well—and he did something just a little extra.

I'm Bob Grant, which of course you have guessed by now. Peter Torrence—the third member of our party—is in the Federal Prison up the Hudson. I had to turn him in.

We were given one of the smaller types of the Bentley—T-44— an alumite cylindrical hull, double-shelled, with the Erentz pressure-current circulating in it. It was a modern, well-equipped little space-ship. In its thirty-foot length of double-decked interior we three were entirely comfortable.... The voyage, past the orbit of Venus and then Mercury as we headed directly for the Sun—using the Sun's full attraction—was amazingly swift and devoid of incident beyond normal space-flight routine. Much of our time was spent in the little forward control turret—the "green-house," where below, above and to the sides the great glittering abyss of the firmament is spread out in all its amazing glory.

Vulcan, if it existed, would be almost directly behind the Sun now. We had no possible chance of sighting it, we knew, even when, heading inward, we cut the orbit of Mercury. Torrence, almost from the start of the trip, figured we should follow into the attraction of Mercury which was then far to one side.

"From that angle we'll see Vulcan just that much sooner," he argued.

"They told me to head straight in, to twenty-nine million miles," I said. "And that's what I'm doing—obeying orders."

I held our plotted course. Torrence never ceased grumbling about it, and I must admit there was a lot of sense in his argument. He is a big fellow—burly, heavy-set and about my own height, which is six feet one. He had close-clipped hair and a square, heavy face. He's just turned thirty, I understand. That's five years older than I— and I was in charge. Perhaps that irked him. He is unquestionably a headstrong fellow; self-confident. But he obeyed orders, though with grumbling. And as a mechanical technician—no one could do better. He knew the technical workings of the little ship inside out.

"We follow orders?" young Jan Holden said. "And when we reach twenty-nine million miles from the Sun—then we're on our own?"

"Yes," I agreed.

"Then, when we head off to round the Sun, if Vulcan is where they think it is we ought to sight it in a few days?"

"I certainly hope so, Jan."

"I wonder if it's inhabited. I wish it would be." His dark eyes were shining. His thin cheeks, usually pale, were flushed with excite- ment. He was just eighteen—only a month past the legal minimum age for Interplanetary employment. A slim, romantic-looking boy, he was willing and eager to help in every way. A good cook, expert in handling his cramped quarters and preparing the many synthetic foods with which we were equipped.

"You hope it's inhabited, Jan?" I asked.

"I sure do."

I grinned at him. "Well, if it is, you'll be disappointed to find I'll be doing my best to keep away from whatever living creatures are there. That's a job for a larger expedition than ours."

"Yes, I suppose it is."

* * * *

Jan often sat with me through our long vigils up there in the green-house. Sometimes he wouldn't speak for an hour—just sitting there dreaming. Sometimes he would talk of the ill-fated Roberts and King Expedition—the only exploratory flight which ever had headed in this close to the Sun. That was five years ago. Roberts and King, with a crew of eight, had never been heard from since.

"I just think they found Vulcan," Jan said once, out of one of his long silences.

"They were told to return after a routine landing," Torrence put in.

"Well then, suppose they crashed their ship," Jan said. "Suppose they can't get back—"

"What we ought to do is sight Vulcan, round it and go home," Torrence said. "To the devil with orders to land. I'd go back and tell them that in my judgment—"

"We'll land," I said. "Determine gravity—meteorological conditions—secure samples of soil, vegetation—what-nots—you know the specifications, Torrence."

If indeed there was any Vulcan. If a landing upon what might be a fiery surface were physically possible....

Another day passed. And then another and another. We were all three tense, expectant. There was little apparent motion in the great starry cyclorama spread around us—just the slow dwindling of Earth and Venus, the monstrous Sun shifting slowly to the right with the starfield behind it progressively becoming visible.

"We're chasing a phantom," Torrence said, on the fourth day, with the Sun now almost abreast of us and some twenty-four million miles distant. "This damned heat! They sent us out for a salary that's a mere pittance—and give us inadequate equipment. No wonder there's been no exploration so close in here."

Bathed in the full, direct Sun-rays our interior air had heated into a torrid swelter. Stripped to the waist, with the sweat glistening on us, we sat in the shrouded green-house.... And then at last I saw Vulcan! A little round, lead-colored blur. Just a dot, but in a few hours it was clear of the intervening Sun. No question of its identity. Vulcan. The new world.

"We did it!" Jan murmured. "Oh, we did it."

* * * *

It was a busy time, for me especially, those next ninety-six hours. I was soon enabled to calculate, at least roughly, that Vulcan was a world of some eight hundred miles diameter, with an orbit approximately eighteen million miles from the Sun.

"It has an atmosphere?" Jan murmured anxiously.

"Yes, I think so." We kept away from the Sun for a time; and then at last we were able to head directly for Vulcan.

The atmosphere presently was visible. No need for us to use the pressure-suits. I envisaged at first that upon such a little world gravity would be very slight. But now the heavy, metallic quality of its rock-surface was apparent. A world, doubtless much denser than igneous Earth.

It was my plan to land on the side away from the Sun.

We rounded Vulcan at some two million miles out. The clouds were fairly dense in many places; sluggish, slow-moving. There were fires on the Sun side—a temperature there which would make it certainly uninhabitable to any creatures resembling humans....

It was the ninth day after the sighting of Vulcan that quite by chance I discovered its *allurite*. We were now fairly close over the dark hemisphere, with the Sun occulted behind it. At a thousand miles of altitude, we were dropping slowly down upon the spreading dark disc which now occupied most of our lower firmament. I had been making a series of routine spectro-color-graphs to file with my reports.

Jan heard my muttered exclamation and came crowding to gaze over my shoulder at the dripping little color spectrograph.

"What is it, Bob? Something important?"

"That bond-line there—see it? That's a metal on Vulcan—shining of its own light—radioactive type-A."

That much, I could determine. Then Jan and I looked it up in the Hughson list of Identified Spectrae. It was *allurite*.

"That's valuable?" Torrence murmured. "Pure *allurite*—"

I laughed. "It certainly would be, if we could find any sizable deposits here. On Earth, it takes some seventeen tons of the very richest *allurium* to get maybe a grain of pure *allurite*. We'll take a look around, try and get a sample of the ore here. If it pans out rich enough, they can send a well-equipped mining expedition."

"We ought to get a bonus for this," Torrence said. "If you don't tell 'em so, I will."

* * * *

The descent upon Vulcan took another twenty-four hours. Then at last we had passed through a cloud-bank and, at some twenty thousand feet, the new world stretched dark and bleak beneath us. It certainly looked—to Jan's intense disappointment—wholly uninhabited. It was a tumbled, rocky landscape, barren and forbidding. Beneath us there were black ravines and canyons, little jagged peaks and hill-top spires, some of them sharp as needle-points. Off at one of the distant horizons the tiered land, rising up, stretched into the foothills of serrated ranks of mountain peaks which loomed over the jagged dark horizon line.

A great metal desert here. In the fitful starlight, and the mellow light of little crescent Mercury which hung over the mountains like a falling, new moon, the metallic quality of the rock was obvious—sleek, bronzed metal ore, in places polished by erosion so that it shone mirror-like. In other places it was mottled with a greenish cast.

"Well," Jan murmured, "not very hospitable-looking, is it? Don't you suppose there's any moisture, or any vegetation?"

There was no sign of any living creatures beneath us as we drifted diagonally downward. But presently, at lower altitude, I could see gleaming pools of water in the rock-hollows. The remains of a rainstorm here. Then we saw what looked like a great fissure—an open scar rifted in a glistening, polished metallic plateau. Grey-black steam was rising, condensing in the humid night-air. The hidden fires of the bowels of the little planet seemed close at this one point. As we stared, a red glow for a moment tinged the steam with a red and greenish reflection of some subterranean glare, far down.

Nothing but metal desert. But presently, as we slid forward, no more than a few thousand feet above the rocky surface now, Jan murmured suddenly,

"Look off there. Like a little oasis, isn't it?"

There was a patch of what seemed to be rocky soil. Just a few hundred acres in extent, set in a cup-like depression with little buttes and needle-spires and the strewn boulders of the metal waste surrounding it. A clump of tangled vegetation covered it—a fantastic miniature jungle of interlaced, queerly shaped little trees, solid with air-vines and pods and clumps of monstrous, vivid-colored flowers. It was an amazing contrast to the bleakness of the bronze desert.

"Well, that's more like it," Jan exclaimed. "Not all desert, Bob. See that?"

Torrence, with his usual efficient practicality, had been busy getting our landing equipment in order. He paused beside me in the green-house, where I sat at the rocket-stream controls which now were in operation for this atmospheric flight.

"Where you figure on landing?" he asked. "Somewhere about here? You want to locate that *allurite*?"

"Yes," I agreed.

* * * *

It is not altogether safe, handling even so small a space-flight ship as ours, in atmosphere at low altitudes. Especially over unknown terrain. It seemed my best course now to make the landing here, secure my rock-samples and make my routine observations. I did not need Torrence to tell me that we were not equipped for extensive exploration of an unknown world. A trip on foot of perhaps a day or two, using the spaceship as a base, would suffice for my records.

"There's a better chance of finding sizable deposits of allurium here than anywhere else?" Torrence suggested. "Don't you think so?"

With that, too, I agreed. He prepared us for a night and a few meals of camping—a huge pack for himself, which with a grin he declared himself amply able to carry; a smaller one for Jan; and my instruments and electro-mining drills for me.

We dropped down within an hour or two, landing with a circular swing into a dim, cauldron-like depression of the desert where the polished ground was nearly level and free of boulders.

That was a thrill to me—my first step into the new world—even though I have experienced it several times before. Laden with our packs, we opened the lower-exit pressure porte. The night air, under heavier pressure than we were maintaining inside, oozed in with a little hiss—moist, queer-smelling air. It seemed at first heavy, oppressive. The acrid smell of chemicals was in it.

The night-temperature was hot—sultry as a summer tropic night on Earth. With the interior gravity shut off as we opened the porte, at once I felt a sense of lightness. But it was not extreme. Despite Vulcan's small size, its great density gives it a gravity comparable to Earth's.

In a little group we stood on the rocky ground with a dark, immense heavy silence around us—a silence that you could seem to hear—and yet a silence which seemed pregnant with the mystery of the unknown. Somehow it made me suddenly think of weapons. Besides our utility-knives, we each had a small, short-range electro-flash gun. I saw that Torrence had his in his hand.

"Put it away," I said. "There's nothing here."

With a grin, he shoved it back into his belt. "Which way?" he demanded. "What will the ore of *allurium* look like? Green and red spots in sand-colored streaks of rock, that Hughson book says."

I figured that I could recognize it, though I am far from a skilled geologist. Certainly I agreed with Torrence that our most important job was to find some sizable lodes of *allurium*, measure its probable extent, and take average samples of it back with us.

* * * *

We climbed out of the little cauldron. In the tumbled darkness we picked our way among the crags. An Earth-mile, then another. Little Jan, like an eager hound was generally ahead of us, with his tiny search-glare sweeping the jagged rocks. We crossed a narrow winding canyon, inspected a slashed cliff-face. It was arduous going. Despite the sense of lightness and our tropic black-drill clothes of short trousers, thin jackets and shirts, we were panting, bathed in sweat within an hour. Silently, Torrence plodded at my side. It was my first trip with him; and I could see he did not altogether trust my efficiency.

"You can find the way back to the ship?" he demanded once. "To get lost in a place like this—"

I had marked it; little twin spires above the cauldron. They were visible now, looming against the dark sky behind us.

I showed him. "I saw them," he said. "I could lead us back. My idea is, if we cover about ten miles and then camp—"

A cry from Jan interrupted us. He was standing on a little ridge of rock like a bronze metal wave frozen into solidity. Against the deep purple sky his slim figure was a silhouette of solid black. He was staring off into the distance; his arm waved with a gesture as he called to us.

"Something off there! Something lying on the rocks—come look!"

We ran to join him. About a quarter mile distant there was a broad gully. A dark blob was visible lying at the bottom of it—a sizable blob, something forty or fifty feet long. We picked our way there; climbed down into the ragged, thirty-foot ravine. It was a spaceship lying here—with its sleek alumite hull resting on its side with one of its rocket-stream fins bent and smashed under it.

"The Roberts-King ship," Torrence exclaimed. "So they got here. Cracked up in the landing."

There seemed no doubt of it. This was unquestionably the Roberts-King vehicle—an older version of our own vessel. We stood staring at it blankly—at its little bow pressure port which was wide open, a narrow rectangle with the interior blackness behind it.

Then I saw that here on the rocks near the doorway, a litter of tools and mechanisms were strewn; and a section of one of the gravity plates which had been disconnected and brought out here.

"Trying to repair it," I said to the silently staring, awed Torrence. "Five years ago. Now what do you suppose—"

A startled cry from Jan interrupted me.

The body was lying on the rocks, just beyond the bow of the ship. It was Jonathan Roberts—stocky, middle-aged leader of the expedition. Clad in a strange costume of thin brown material, seemingly animal skin, he lay crumpled. I had never met him, but from his published portraits I could recognize him at once. In the starlight here his dead face with staring eyes goggled up at us.

"Why—why—" Torrence gasped. "Five years—"

There was no great look of decay about the body. Roberts had died here, certainly not five years ago. I was bending down over the body; I shoved at one of the shoulders and turned it over. Stricken Jan, Torrence and I stared numbed. A thin bronze sliver of metal—fin-tipped like a metal arrow—was buried in Roberts' back!

Again the alert Jan was gazing at the dim, fantastic night-scene around us. Abruptly his hand gripped my arm as he gasped,

"Why—good Lord—what's that? Over there—"

In the blackness down the gully, perhaps a hundred feet from us, a little spiral of fire had appeared. A tiny wisp of red-green flame. It seemed to hover in the air a few feet above the rocky gully floor. Like a phantom wraith of fire, it silently leaped and twisted.

"My God—it's coming toward us!" Torrence suddenly gasped.

In the darkness the silent wisp of fire had swayed sidewise, and then came along the edge of the gully, a disembodied conflagration in mid-air, as though wafted by a rush of wind we could not feel.

CHAPTER II

For a moment of startled horror we stood motionless. The floating little flame seemed bounding now, just over the rocks. Bounding? Abruptly I seemed to see a dark shape of solidity under it—something almost, but not quite invisible in the blackness. A tangible thing? A creature—burning? Thoughts are instant things. I recall that in that second, I had the impression of a four-legged thing like a huge dog, bounding toward us over the rocks. The flame in which it was enveloped, had spread—it was a blob of flame, but solidity was there.

All in a second. My little electro-gun was in my hand. And then from beside me, Torrence fired—his flash with a whining sizzle splitting the blackness of the gully with its pencil-point of hurled electrons. His hasty aim quite evidently was wild. I saw the little splash of colored sparks where his charge hit the rocks. Too high.

My gun was leveled. But in that split-second, the oncoming blob of fire abruptly had been extinguished. There was only the faint blurred suggestion of the dog-like thing. It had stopped short, and then suddenly was retreating. My shot, and Jan's, followed it. In another few seconds there was no possibility of hitting it. Silently it had vanished. There was only the black silent gully around us, with the blurred crags standing like menacing dark ghosts.

My instinct then, I must admit, was for us to retreat at once to our ship. In the heavy empty silence we stood blankly gazing at each other. Torrence was grim; Jan was shaking with excitement and the fear all of us felt.

"You heard that whistle?" I murmured.

"I heard it," Jan exclaimed. "Something—somebody—human—" There were weird, hostile inhabitants on Vulcan—no question of that now! And here was Roberts' body with a metal sliver of arrow in its back, mute evidence of what we were facing. And already our presence here had been discovered. I stared around at the rocky darkness, every blurred crag now seeming to mask some unknown menace.

"That whistle," Torrence murmured, "calling off that flaming thing—started at our shots. Something is around here, watching us now, undoubtedly."

The yawning dark doorway of the wrecked spaceship was near us. Something seemed lying just beyond its threshold.

"You two stay here," I told Torrence and Jan. "Don't let them surprise us again. We'll have to get back to our ship—"

The port doorway led into a little pressure chamber. On its dark sloping floor, as the wrecked ship lay askew, I stood with my flashlight illumining so ghastly a scene that my blood chilled in my veins. It was a bloody shambles of horror. For a moment I gazed; and as I turned away, sickened, I found Jan at my elbow. He too, had been staring. He clutched at me, white and shaken, and I turned away my light.

"The rest of them," he murmured.

"Yes. Looks that way. All of them—"

The bodies were strewn, clothing and flesh ripped apart so that here were only the bones of men, with pulpy crimson—

"No humans did that, Jan."

"No," he shuddered. "That Thing in flames that came at us—"

His words died in his throat. Outside there was a scream—a shrill, eerie human cry. The high-pitched scream of a woman! Gun in hand, with Jan close behind me, I ran outside. The dimness of the rocky gully seemed empty. The cry had died away.

"Torrence! You Torrence—what in the devil—"

My low vehement words wafted away. There was no Torrence. Cautiously I ran around the bow of the wrecked ship, gazed down its other side.

"Torrence—Torrence—"

The nearby rocks seemed to echo back my words, mocking me.

"Why—why—" Jan gasped, "I left him right out here. He was just standing, looking down at Roberts' body with the arrow in it. I just thought I'd go inside with you for a minute."

I pulled him down to the ground. We crouched, close against the side of the ship. "That scream," I whispered, "wasn't far away. A few hundred feet down the gully."

"It sounded like a girl. It did, didn't it? Bob, if they got Torrence that quickly—an arrow in him—"

I peered, tense. The rock shadows were all motionless. In the heavy blank silence there was only my startled breathing, and Jan's; and the thumping of my own heart against my ribs. Had this weird enemy gotten Torrence so swiftly, so silently? Something not human, that had so quickly seized him and dragged him away? Or one of those metal arrows in his back, so that his body was lying around here somewhere, masked by the darkness. Jan and I had certainly not been inside the ship more than a minute or two—

A sharp clattering ping against the alumite side of the wrecked ship struck away my thoughts. A metal arrow! It bent against the hull-plate and dropped almost beside me! The still-hidden sniper had seen us, that was evident, for the arrow had whizzed only a foot or so over our heads.

"Jan—lower—"

We almost flattened ourselves against the bulge of the hull, with a little pile of boulders in front of us. My gun was leveled, but there was nothing to shoot at. Then from diagonally across the gully again there came a sharp human cry! A girl's voice? It was soft this time, a bursting little cry, half suppressed.

Thoughts are instant things. I was aware of the cry and with it there was another whizz. Another arrow. This one was wider of the mark; it hit far to one side of us, up near the bow of the ship.

"Jan! Wait!" His little flash gun was up in the crevice of the rocks in front of us. In another second he would have fired. I saw his target—two dim blobs across the gully. For just that second they were visible as they rose up out of a hollow. A man; and the slighter figure with him seemed that of a girl. Her hair, glistening like spun metal in the dim light, hung over her shoulders.

The two figures were struggling. There was the sound of the girl's low cry, and a grunt from the man.... My low admonition stopped Jan from firing and in another second the shapes across the gully had vanished.

"That girl," I murmured. "She tried to keep him from killing us. Seemed that way, don't you think?"

"Well—"

* * * *

We waited. From across the gully there was no sound. I could see now that there was a little ridge in the broken, littered gully floor, behind which the two figures had vanished. A lateral depression was there, with the ragged, broken cliff-wall some ten feet behind it.

"Do you suppose there's only one of them?" Jan whispered. "One man—and that girl—"

"And that—that Thing in flames—"

There was no sign of the animal-like creature. For another moment we crouched tense, peering, listening. A loose stone the size of my fist was here beside us. I picked it up. It was weirdly heavy for its size. Then I flung it out into the gully to the right of us. It fell with a clatter.

Our enemy was there all right. An arrow whizzed in the darkness and struck near where the stone had fallen.

Jan laughed with contempt. "Dumb enough—that fellow. Bob, listen, we've got flash-guns. That fellow with no brains—and just with arrows—"

True enough. "You stay here," I whispered.

"What's the idea?"

"You wait a couple of minutes. Then throw another stone off to the right—about the same place. Understand?"

"No, I don't."

"Well, you do it, anyhow."

There seemed a line of shadow to the left of us, a shadow which extended well out into the gully. The ground dropped down in that area—a slope strewn with crags, broken with little crevices. Crouching low, I crept to the bow of the ship, to the left away from Jan; sank down, waited. There was no sound; evidently I had not been seen. I started again, picking my way down the slope.

A minute. I was well out into the gully now, ten feet or so down, so that I could not see the wrecked ship where Jan was crouching. From here the opposite cliff-wall showed dark and ragged. Occasionally it yawned with openings, like little cave-mouths. The place where the figures had been crouching should be visible from here. The broken, lower side of the little ridge behind which they had dropped was in view to me now. It was dark with shadow, but there seemed nothing there.

Slowly, cautiously, I crossed the gully. Two minutes since I had left Jan? I melted down beside a rock, almost at the edge of the cliff-wall. And then, out in the gully, far to the right, I heard the stone clatter as Jan threw it.

There was no answering arrow-shot this time.... One can be very incautious, usually at just the wrong moment. I recall that I stood up to see better, though I flattened myself against a boulder. And suddenly, close behind me, I was aware of a padding, thudding rhythmic sound on the rocks. I whirled. I had only a second's vision of a dark bounding animal shape coming at me. My sizzling little flash went under it as it rose in one of its bounding leaps.

I had no time to fire another shot. Frantically I pulled the trigger-lever, but the gun's voltage had not yet rebuilt to firing pressure. Futilely I flung the gun into the creature's face as it bore down upon me.

The impact of the dark oblong body knocked me backward so that I fell with it sprawling, snarling upon me. In the chaos of my mind there was only the dim realization of a heavy body as big as my own; spindly legs, like the legs of a huge dog. There seemed six or eight legs, scrambling on me.

Wildly I fought to heave it off. There was a face—a ring of glaring green eyes; fang-like jaws of a long pointed snout which opened, snarling with a gibbering, gruesome cry. I shoved my left forearm into the jaws as they came at my face. They closed upon my arm, ripping, tearing.

* * * *

But somehow I was aware that I had lunged to my feet. And the Thing reared up with me. It was a Thing almost as heavy as myself. My left arm had come loose from its jaws and as its scrambling weight pressed me I went down again. A Thing of rubber? It seemed boneless, the shape of it bending as I seized it. A gruesomely yielding body. My flailing blows bounded back from it. Then I knew that I was gripping it by the head, twisting it. The snarling, snapping jaws suddenly opened wide with a scream—a scream that faded into a mouthing gibber, and in my grip the Thing went limp. I cast it away and it sank to the rocks, quivering.

For an instant I stood panting, trembling with nausea sickening me. On my hands the flesh of the weird antagonist was sticking like viscous, gluey rubber. Hot and clinging. Hot? I stared at my hands in the dimness. For a second I thought it was phosphorescence. Then yellow-green wisps of flame were rising from my hands. Frantically I plunged them into my jacket pockets. The tiny flames were extinguished. I stripped off my jacket, flung it away and it lay with a little smoke rising from it where the weird stuff was trying again to burst into flame.

The skin of my hands was seared, but the contact with the flames had been only momentary and the burns were not severe. It had all happened in a minute or two. I recall that I was standing trembling, staring at the yawning mouth of a cave entrance which was nearby in the cliff-face. A movement in there? A moving blob? Then I was aware that there was a light behind me. Off across the gully there was a blob of light-fire. A red-green blob, swirling, scrambling. And the sound of a distant, gibbering snarl....

The singing whizz of an arrow past my head made me turn again. My human adversary! I saw him now. He was coming at a run from the mouth of the cave—a wide-shouldered, grotesquely-shaped man with a brown hairy garment draped upon him. He swayed like a gorilla on thick bent legs. In one hand he held what seemed an arrow-sling. In the other he carried a long narrow segment of rock, swinging it like a club. He was no more than ten feet from me. In the dimness I could see his huge round head with tangled, matted blank hair. As I whirled to meet him, his voice was a bellow of guttural roar, like an animal bellowing to intimidate its enemy.

I turned, jumped sidewise. And abruptly from a rock-shadow another shape rose up! Slim, small white body, brown-draped with long, gleaming tawny hair. The girl! Her voice gasped,

"You run! He kill you! In here—this way—"

The bellowing savage had turned heavily in his rush and was charging us. In her terror and confusion the girl gripped me, shoving me toward the cave. As we ran I flung an arm around her, lifting her up. She weighed hardly more than a child. Then we were in the blackness of a tunnel-passage. I set her down.

"Lie down. Be quiet," I whispered vehemently. She understood me; she crouched back against the side wall. There seemed a little light here, a glow which I realized was inherent to the rocks, like a vague, faint phosphorescence. But it was brighter outside. The charging savage had evidently paused at the entrance. As I stared now, his bulky figure loomed there, grotesque silhouette. Then doubtless he saw me. With another bellow he came charging in.

I stood waiting, like a Toreador, in front of a heavily charging bull. It was something like that, for as he rushed me, swinging his club and plunging with lowered head of matted hair, nimbly I jumped aside. I had seized a rock half as big as my head. He had no time to turn and poise himself as I jumped on him, crashing the rock at the side of his broad ugly face as he straightened and swung around.

Ghastly blow. His face smashed in as the rock seemed to go into it. For a second his hulking body stood balanced upon the crooked legs and broad flat bare feet. Gruesome dead thing with the face and top of the head gone, it balanced on legs suddenly turned rigid. Then it toppled forward and thudded against the passage wall, sliding sidewise to the ground where it lay motionless.

* * * *

In the phosphorescent dimness, I dropped beside the girl. She was panting with terror, shuddering, with her hands before her face.

"It's all right," I murmured. "Or at least, maybe it isn't all right with you, but he's dead, anyway."

Utterly incongruous, the delicately formed bronze-white girl—and that hulking, grotesque, clumsy savage.

"Oh—yes," she murmured. "Dear—yes—"

"You speak English—strange, here on Vulcan—"

"But from your Captain Roberts—he was the fren' of mine—of all the Senzas—"

"He's dead. An arrow in him—lying over there by his wrecked ship—the rest of them, dead inside—"

"Yes. I know it. That was these Orgs. I was caught—just the last time of sleep. Tahg—surely it seems it must be Tahg who sent this Org to take me from my father's home—"

A captive! And she had fought with her savage captor to stop him from sending an arrow into me. Then, in his absorption as he tried to stalk me, she had broken loose from him.

"Just this one Org?" I murmured. "Is he the only one around here? He and that—animal-thing which I killed?"

"That—a female *mime*—you—you—"

She was huddling beside me, clinging to me, still shuddering. "Two Orgs there were," she whispered. "And another mime—a fire-male—"

The flame-creature! Queerly, it was not until that instant that I thought of Jan. Out there across the gully, that swirling swaying blob of light-fire! Those snarling sounds! Jan had been attacked by another of the savages, and by the weird flaming creature! The mime fire-male, as the girl called it.

I jumped to my feet. "What—what you do?" she demanded.

"You stay here. What's your name?"

"Ama. Daughter of Rohm, the Senza. He my father. He very good fren' of the Captain Roberts—good fren' of all the Earthmen. Like you? You are Earthman?"

"Yes. Now Ama, listen—I came here with another Earthman— with two others, in fact. One of them is over there by the Roberts' ship.... You wait here—"

"No!" she gasped. I had dashed toward the tunnel entrance, but I found her with me. "No—no, I stay with you."

From the entrance the gully showed dim and silent. Over the little rise of ground, just the top of the Roberts' spaceship was visible.

Ama clung to me. "I stay with you," she insisted.

Cautiously we picked our way across the gully, up the small ascending slope. No sound; nothing moving. But now there was a pungent, acrid chemical smell hanging here in the windless air.

"The fire-mime!" Ama whispered. "You smell the fire? Then he was angry, ready to fight—"

"He fought," I retorted grimly. "I saw it—"

"Look! Look there—"

* * * *

Her slim arm as she gestured tinkled with metal baubles hanging on it.... I saw, up the slope, the blob of something lying on the rocks. Jan! My heart pounded. But it wasn't Jan. The body of one of the weird oblong animals was lying there. Lying on its side, with its six legs stiffly outstretched. Ugly hairless thing, like a giant dog which had been skinned. I could see now that the grey-green flesh had a greasy, pulpy look. What strange organic material was this? Certainly nothing like it existed on Earth. Impervious to heat, as the human stomach tissue is impervious to the action of its own digestive juices. Evidence of the thing's flaming oxidation was here. Wisps of smoke were rising from the ground about the slack body.

Had Jan killed it? The ring of eyes above the long muzzle snout bulged with a glassy, goggling dead stare. The jaws were open, with a thick, forked black tongue protruding, and green, sticky-looking froth still oozing out. The teeth were long and sharp, fangs like polished black ivory protruding from the jaw. The cause of its death was obvious. A knife-slash had ripped, almost severed its throat in a hideous wound where green-black viscous ooze was still slowly dripping, with smoky vapor rising from it.

For a moment, with little Ama clinging to me, I must have stood appalled at the weird sight of the dead fire-mime. If Jan had fought and killed it—then where was he now? And where was that other Org, companion of the clumsy savage I had killed when it had tried to attack me?

And where was Torrence?

"Your fren'—he did this?" Ama was murmuring.

"Yes, I guess so." I raised my voice cautiously. "Jan—Oh, Jan, where are you?"

The dark shadowed rocks mocked me with their muffled, blurred echo of my call. There seemed nothing here alive, save Ama and me. The wrecked spaceship lay broken and silent on the rocks, with the gruesome, strewn bodies of the Earthmen in it. And the body of Roberts still lay here outside, near the bow.

"Jan—Jan—"

Then Ama abruptly gasped, "The Orgs! See them—up there!"

The cliff which was the gully wall, at this point was some fifty feet high. I stared up to a patch of yellow light which had appeared there in the darkness. A band of the murderous Orgs! Carrying flaming torches, a dozen or more of the gargoyle savages stood above us on the cliff-brink. One stood in advance of them, pointing down at us.

He was the other one, doubtless, who had originally been down here with Ama. Around them, half a dozen of the huge greenish mimes bounded, whining with gibbering cries of eagerness.

And in that instant, an arrow came down. I saw one of the savages sling it from a flexible, whip-like contrivance. The whizzing metal shaft sang past our heads and clattered on the rocks.

Ama was clutching me. "You come! Oh hurry—they kill us both."

There was no argument about that. I flung a last look around with the vague thought that I would see Jan lying here. Then I let Ama guide me. At a run, we headed back down the declivity and diagonally across the gully. A rain of arrows came down, clattering around us, but in a moment most of them were falling short.

"Which way, Ama? Where we go?"

"My people—my village—not too far."

"Which way?"

"Through this cliff. There are passages into the lower valley."

"You know the way?"

"Yes, oh yes."

A dark opening in the opposite cliff presently was before us. The Orgs were coming down the other cliff now; their bellowing voices and the whining cries of the mimes were a blended babble.

"A storm is coming," Ama said suddenly.

The distant sky over the lower end of the gully was shot now with weird lurid colors. In the heavy dark silence here around us, a sudden sharp puff of wind plucked at us, tossing Ama's long tawny hair.

"This way—" she added.

My arm went around her as another wind-blast thrust us sidewise, almost knocking her off her feet. Then clinging together, fighting our way in a rush of wind which now abruptly was a roar, we plunged into the depths of the yawning tunnel.

CHAPTER III

I must recount now what happened to Jan, as he told it to me when after a sequence of weird events, he and I were together again. When I left him crouching there close against the hull of the wrecked Roberts' ship, he lost sight of me almost in a moment. There was just the faint blob of me sliding into a shadow; and then the lowering ground down which I went hid me. Tensely he crouched, peering across the gully, listening to the heavy silence.

Two minutes, I had said; and then he must throw the rock. His hand fumbled around, found a sizable rock-chunk. He understood my purpose, of course—to divert our adversary across the gully at a moment when I might be close to jump him from the other direction.

Jan was excited, apprehensive, just an inexperienced boy. Was the crouching savage with the girl still there across the gully? There was no sound, no movement. Was it two minutes now?

He flung the stone at last and raised himself up a little with his gun leveled. The stone clattered off to the right. But it provoked no whizzing arrow. No sound of me, jumping upon my adversary.... Nothing.... But what was that? Jan stiffened. Distinctly he heard the sizzling puff of a flashgun shot. My gun! He knew it must be; it was to the left, out in the gully. And following it there was a low gibbering snarl. Faint in the distance, but in the heavy silence plainly audible.

I had been attacked! Jan found himself on his feet, with no thought in his mind save to dash to me.... He had taken no more than a few scrambling leaps on the rocks. He reached the brink of the descent. Far down and out in the gully it seemed that he could see the blur of something fighting.

His low incautious movement had betrayed him. From behind him there was a low whistling. A signal! An eager whining snarl instantly resounded to it. Jan had no more than time to whirl and face the sounds when a great bounding grey-green shape was on him!

Jan's shot missed it, and the next second the lunging oblong body struck him. The impact knocked him backward. His gun clattered away. Then the huge, hairless dog-like thing sprawled upon him, its slavering jaws snapping. They found his shoulder as he lunged and the fang-like teeth sank in....

A miracle that Jan could have kept his wits so that he fumbled for his knife as he fell. But suddenly he got it out, stabbed and slashed wildly with it as he rolled and twisted on the ground with the snarling creature on top of him.... And suddenly he was aware that the thing had burst into flame!

It could have been only a few seconds during which Jan fought that weird living fire. It was a wild chaos of horror.... Licking, oozing flames exuding like an aura from the sticky viscous flesh that horribly sprawled upon him. Monstrous ghastly adversary, with flesh that seemed now like burning bubbling rubber, stenching with acrid gas-fumes....

Just a few seconds, then Jan realized that somehow he had broken loose from the jaws that gripped his shoulder. He tried to scramble to his feet. The flames searing his face made him close his eyes. He was holding his breath, choking. His clothes were on fire....

* * * *

Then the sprawling, lunging body knocked him down again. He was still wildly, blindly slashing with his knife. Vaguely he was aware, over the chaos of snapping snarls, that a human voice nearby with guttural shouts was urging the animal to dispatch its victim. But suddenly—as Jan's knife-blade ripped into its throat—the snarls went into a ghastly, eerie animal scream of agony—a long scream that died into a gurgle of gluey, choking blood-fluid....

Jan was aware that the creature had fallen from him with its flames dying. On the rocks he rolled away from it, with his scorched hands wildly brushing his clothes to extinguish them. Then he was on his feet, staggering, choking, coughing. But his knife, its blade dripping with an oozing flame, still wildly waved.

And then he was aware that twenty feet away, a heavy, grotesque man-like shape was standing with a club and arrow-sling. But with his flame-creature dead and the sight of the staggering, triumphant Jan waving his flaming knife-blade—the watching savage suddenly dropped his club and let out a cry of dismay and fear. And then he ran.

For a moment Jan, wildly, hysterically laughing, went in pursuit. But in the rocky darkness the fleeing savage already had vanished....

Then reaction set in upon Jan. His burned face and hands stung as though still fire was upon him. He was still gasping, choking from the fumes of his smoldering clothes. His eyes, with lashes singed, smarted, watering so that all the vague night-scene was a swaying blur.... He found himself sitting down on the rocks....

And then suddenly he remembered me. Where had I gone? What had happened?...

Vaguely Jan recalled that I had left him and gone across the gully.... Where was I now?... Then he seemed dimly to recall that he had heard my shot....

In the dimness suddenly it seemed to Jan that he saw me, far up the gully to the right, up on the cliff-top. For just a moment he was sure that it was the shape of me, silhouetted against the sky.... The sight gave him strength. Still staggering, he ran wildly forward.... A quarter of a mile; certainly it seemed that far. He had crossed the gully by now. The figure up above had vanished.... Queer. What was I doing up there? Chasing the savage?...

Jan climbed the little cliff, which was ragged, and lower here than elsewhere. It led him to the undulating, upper plateau, crag-strewn, dim under a leaden sky. But there was enough light so that he could see the distant figure. It was only two or three hundred yards away, plodding on, apparently not looking back....

Jan ran after it. And then he was calling:

"Bob! You Bob—"

The figure turned. Started suddenly back, and called:

"Is that you? Jan?"

It was Torrence! He came back at a lumbering run now—Torrence, bare-headed, gun in hand. But he obviously hadn't had any encounter. His jacket was buttoned across his shirt; he looked just as he had when Jan had last seen him, out there at the bow of the wrecked spaceship when Jan had gone inside to join me.

Torrence stared at the burned Jan. "Why—good Heavens," he gasped. "You—I saw that thing killing you. I was up here—I started down, but too late—"

"Where's Bob?"

"Bob? Why—he was killed. Burned—like you. I tried to help him—too late—the damned things—"

* * * *

The lameness of it was lost on the still-dazed Jan at that moment. I had been killed! It struck him with a shock. And as he stood wavering, trembling, Torrence drew him to a rock.

"Too bad," Torrence murmured sympathetically.

"Where—where were you?" Jan said at last. "We came out of the ship—couldn't find you."

"I was attacked by one of those cursed Things. Like the one that nearly got you—like the one that killed Bob. I chased it; shot at it when I got up here. But I shouldn't have come up—then I saw you and Bob—too late to get back to you. So I was starting for our ship. It's off this way, not so very far."

For a little time Jan sat there numbed, and Torrence sat sympathetically, silently beside him.

"When we get back," Torrence murmured at last, "you can put in your report with mine. We did our best—but there isn't any use now, us tackling this thing."

Jan must have been wholly silent, thinking of me, dead, burned, back there in the darkness of the gully.

"You all right now, lad?"

"Yes," Jan said. "Yes—I'm all right."

"When we get back, we ought to get a bonus," Torrence said. "Don't worry, Jan—I'll see you get plenty. Your report and mine—to tell them the hazards of this trip—"

"We should go back?" Jan said.

"Yes, certainly we should. Get back to Earth as fast as we can. No chance of doing anything else—"

Torrence gazed apprehensively around them in the darkness. That much at least—the reality of his apprehension as they sat there on the open plateau—that was authentic enough. And Jan also felt that at any moment one of the flaming creatures might attack them.

"You strong enough to start now?"

"Yes, sure I am," Jan agreed.

They started, picking their way along. Jan tried to remember how far we three had come from our own ship until we had discovered the Roberts' vessel.... For ten or fifteen minutes now he and Torrence clambered over the rocks.

"You think you know the way?" Jan asked at last.

"Yes—or I thought I did." Torrence's tone was apprehensively dubious. And that, too must have been authentic. Certainly it would be a desperate plight to be lost here on Vulcan. "It was Bob who was sure he knew the way back—"

"I think we are all right," Jan agreed. "That big rock-spire off there—I remember it."

As they progressed, Jan was aware now that the sky behind them was brightening. They turned and stared at it.

"Weird—" Torrence muttered.

"Yes—some sort of storm. If it's bad—you suppose we ought to take shelter? It's pretty open up here."

The sky was certainly weird enough—a swirl of leaden clouds back there, shot now with lurid green and crimson. And suddenly there came a puff of wind. Then another. Stronger, it whined between the nearby naked crags. In a little nearby ravine it caught an area of loose metallic stones, whirled them before it with a tinkling clatter.

"We came through that ravine, coming out this way," Jan said suddenly. "I'm sure of it."

Torrence remembered it also. Another blast of wind came; and with it blowing them, they scurried into the ravine. The lurid storm-sky painted it with a crimson and green glare, so that the narrow cut in the rocky plateau was eerie. To Jan it seemed suddenly infernal. He clutched at the larger, far more bulky Torrence as they hurried along with the wind blasting them.

Loose metallic stones were blowing around them now with a clatter. Then suddenly the sky seemed riven by a darting, jagged red shaft of lightning. And then red rain was pelting them.

"Got to find some place," Torrence panted. He had to shout it above the roar as the wind tore at his words and hurled them away.

"Over there?" Jan gestured. "Looks like a cave."

The sides of the ravine were rifted in many places with vertical crevices. They headed toward a wider slit of opening which seemed to lead well back underground. A place of shelter until this storm passed....

* * * *

To Jan, what happened then was weirdly terrifying. He suddenly realized that as they approached the opening, they were being pulled at it. Into it! A suction, as though somewhere down underground this storm had created a partial vacuum—a far lesser pressure so that the air of the little ravine was rushing into it!

Terrified, both of them now were fighting to keep away. But it was no use. Like wind-blown puffs of cotton they were sucked into the yawning opening. A sudden chaos of roaring horror. Jan felt that he was still clutching at Torrence. Then both of them fell, sliding, sucked forward as a plunger cylinder is sucked through a pneumatic tube. The ground here in the passage felt smooth as polished marble.

For how long they plunged forward Jan had no conception. Roaring, sucking darkness. Then it seemed that there was a little light. An effulgence; a pallid, eerie glow, like phosphorescence streaming from the rocks. The narrow passage was steadily widening; and then abruptly they were blown out into emptiness.

It was a vast grotto, with smooth metallic floor almost level. The effulgence here was brighter, so that an undulating, vaulted ceiling glistened far overhead. For a moment the nearer wall was visible, smooth, burnished metal rock. Eroded by the winds of centuries, all the rock here was burnished until it shone mirror-like.

The huge pallid interior roared and echoed with the tumbling wind-torrents seething in it. A lashing cauldron jumbled with eddying blasts. Jan and Torrence tried to get to their feet. They could see now that they were far out from the wall—sliding, buffeted, desperately clinging together, hurled one way and then another. Bruised from head to foot, panting, gasping in the swiftly changing pressures, Jan felt his senses leaving him. A numbed vagueness was on him, so that there was only the suck and roar of the winds and the feel of Torrence to whom he was clinging. They were lying prone now—

"Easing up a little—" He heard Torrence's voice as though from far away. And then he came to his senses to find that he and Torrence had hit against a wall of the grotto and were clinging to a projection of rock.

Easing up a little.... The storm outside lessening.... Jan must have drifted off again; and after another interval he was conscious that there was only a tossing, crazy breeze in here. It whined and moaned, echoing from one wall to another so that the pallid, silvery half-light seemed filled with a myriad gibbering little voices.

And Jan could see now that he and Torrence had been blown into a recess of the grotto—a smaller cave. The rock formation here was as though this were the heart of a monstrous crystal—vertical facets of strata that glistened pallidly.

"We'll have to try and cross back," Torrence said, and in the confined space his words weirdly echoed, split and duplicated so that there seemed many little whispering replicas of his words. "Find that passage where we came in—"

They were on their feet now—suddenly to Jan there was around them a vast vista of pallid dimness. A glowing, limitless abyss stretching off into shadowy nothingness, everywhere he looked.

"Why—why," he murmured, "this place—so large—"

Torrence still had his flash cylinder. He fumbled in his jacket pocket, brought it out. Amazing thing! As he snapped it on, its tiny white beam showed mirrored in a hundred places of the paneled, crystalline walls! The blurred image of Torrence and Jan standing holding each other with their light-shaft before them, duplicated so that there were a hundred of them everywhere they looked! And countless other hundreds smaller and smaller in the myriad backgrounds!

* * * *

With a startled curse Torrence took a few steps into what seemed pallid emptiness, and then suddenly his image was coming at him! Lost! To Jan came the rush of horror that they might, wander in here, balked at every turn....

Another startled cry from Torrence stuck away Jan's thoughts. Neither he nor Torrence had time to make a move. There was suddenly everywhere the duplicated image of a thick, swaying, gargoyle savage, standing like a gorilla on thick bent legs, with one crooked arm holding a flaming torch over his head. A myriad replicas of him everywhere! Was he close to them, or far away? And in which direction?

In that stricken second the questions stabbed into Jan's tumultuous mind. Then he was aware of something whirling in the air over his head—something crashing on his skull so that all the world seemed to go up into a splitting, blinding roar of light. He felt his legs buckling under him. There was only Torrence's fighting outcry and the sound of a guttural echoing voice as Jan fell and his senses slid off into a blank and black, empty silence....

CHAPTER IV

I go back now to that moment when Ama and I, pursued by the roaming band of Orgs, plunged into a tunnel passage that led from the gully, near the wrecked Roberts' spaceship. It was quite evident that Ama was aware of the dangers of the wind-storms of her little world. There was a swift air-current sucking into this passage. But it was not powerful enough to do more than hurry us along. Once, where the tunnel branched, there seemed an open grotto up a little subterranean ascent to the right. It glowed with a brighter pallid light than was here in the passage. I turned that way with an interested gaze, but at once she clutched at me.

"No—no. In times of the storm, very bad sometimes in places under the ground."

There seemed no sign of pursuit behind us. "The Orgs—they run heavy," Ama said when I mentioned it. In the pale opalescent glow of the tunnel, I could see her faint triumphant smile as she gazed up at me sidewise. Strange little face, utterly foreign so that upon Earth, by Earth standards one would have been utterly baffled to identify her. But it was an appealing face, and now, with her terror gone, the sly glance she flung at me was wholly feminine.

"Those fire-mimes," I said. "Couldn't they rush ahead of their masters, trailing us?" I explained how on Earth dogs would do that, following their quarry by the scent. She looked puzzled, and then she brightened.

"I remember. The Captain Roberts told us about that. The mimes are different. The male and female both—they follow what it is they see, nothing else."

Then she told me about the weird, dog-like creatures. The male, exuding a scent—if you could call it that—a vapor which in the air bursts into spontaneous combustion as it combines with the atmospheric oxygen.

How long we ran through what proved to be a maze of passages in the honey-combed ground, I have no idea. Several Earth-miles, doubtless. Several times we stopped to rest, with the breezes tossing about us as I listened, tense, to be sure the Orgs were not coming. Then at last we emerged; and at the rocky exit I stood staring, amazed.

It was a wholly different looking world here. The pallid underground sheen was gone; and now again there was the dim twilight of the interminable Vulcan night. From where we stood the ground sloped down so that we were looking out over the top of a wide spread of lush, tangled forest. Weird jungle, rank and wild with spindly trees of fantastic shapes, heavy with pods and exotic flowers and tangled with masses of vines. Beyond it, far ahead of us there seemed a line of little metal mountains at the horizon; and to the left an Earth-mile or so away, the forest was broken to disclose a winding thread of little river. It shone phosphorescent green in the half light. The storm was over now, but still the colors lingered in the cloud sky—a glorious palette of rainbow hues up there that tinted the forest-top.

Ama gestured toward the thread of river. "The Senzas—my people and my village—off that way beyond the little water. We go quickly. But we be careful, until we get beyond the water."

"Swim it?"

"We can. But I think I remember where there is a Senza boat hidden on this side."

* * * *

She had already told me more of what happened to her. The Senzas, primitive obviously, yet with an orderly tribal civilization, were the dominant race here on little Vulcan. The savage Orgs—a far lower, more primitive type both mentally and physically—in nomadic fashion, roamed the metal deserts and little stunted forests which lay beyond the barren regions. They were, at times of religious frenzy, cannibalistic, with weird and gruesome festival rites which Ama only shudderingly sketched.

For the most part, the clumsy Orgs and their weird mime-creatures were kept from the Senza forests. But occasionally they raided, stealing the Senza women, and roaming the lush forests for food. There had been, in the Senza village, one Tahg, a wooer of Ama. An older man, but somehow well liked by the Senza tribal leader. Repulsed by Ama, he had threatened her—and then he had vanished from the village; gone hunting, and the Senzas considered that the Orgs might have killed him.

"But I think it was Org blood in him," Ama said. "I told the Captain Roberts that—I remember just before he and his men left us to finish the repairs of their ship—and then we found later that the Orgs had killed them all."

Tahg, Ama thought, had become the tribal leader of this group of the Orgs—indulging with them in their gruesome rites.... Then, just a few hours ago, two Orgs had crept upon Ama as she slept—with extraordinary daring for an Org, had successfully seized her and carried her off. Taking her into the Org country, past the Roberts' spaceship, where they had come upon me, and Torrence and Jan....

"We be careful now," she was telling me as we stood gazing out over the forested slope. "After a storm it is when the Orgs mostly roam—the hunting here is better when the little creatures are out after the water."

The little creatures! Best of the animal foods here on Vulcan.... The red-storm quite evidently had emptied torrential rain on the forest. The fantastic trees were heavy with it. Soddenly it dripped from the overhead branches. And now as we started down the slope, I saw the little creatures. Insect or animal, no one could have said. A myriad sizes and shapes of them, from a finger-length to the size of a cat. Before our advance they scurried, on the ground, scattering with weird little outcries. Some flew clumsily into the leaves overhead;

others ran up there on the vines, peering down at us as we passed. We came suddenly upon a pool of rain-water. Greedily a hundred little orange-green things, seemingly almost all head and snout, were crowding at the pool, sucking up the water. With eerie, maniacal little voices they rolled and bounced away at our approach.

This weird forest! Abruptly I was aware that there were places where the rope-like vines and leafy branches of the underbrush shrank away from us as we advanced—slithering and swaying little vines in sudden movement before us. Sentient vegetation. There are plants on Earth which shrink and shudder at a touch. Others which snap and seize an unwary insect enemy. But here it was far more startling than that. I saw a vine on the ground rise up upon its myriad little tendrils; the pods, like a row of heads upon it were quivering, puffing. The extended length of it, like a snake slithered from my threatening tread.

"It fears every human," Ama said. "A strange thing to you Earthmen?"

"Well, slightly," I commented. "Suppose it—some of this vegetation got angry—" Fantastic thought, but the reality of it—a looping, swaying vine over our heads, as thick as my arm—that was a stark reality. "Would a thing like that attack us, Ama?"

She shrugged. "There is talk of it. But I think no one is ever truthful to say it really happened."

We were in the depths of the forest now. In the humid, heavy darkness it was sometimes arduous going. That thread of river—we could not see it now, but I judged it still must be half an Earth-mile away. Once we sat down in a little open glade to rest. In the thick silence the throbbing voice of the forest, blended of the scurrying life and the rustling vines, was a faint steady hum. Then suddenly I saw that Ama was tense, alert, sitting up listening. She looked startled, abruptly frightened.

"What is it?" I whispered.

"Off there—the vines, they are frightened. You hear?"

* * * *

It seemed that somewhere near us, the vine-rustling had grown louder. A scurry, mingled with little popping sounds from the pods. Someone coming? I recall that the startled thought struck me. Then from a thicket near at hand a group of little creatures came dashing. They saw us, wheeled and scurried sidewise. I was on my feet, peering into the shadowed leafy darkness. I thought I heard a low, guttural voice. Whether I did or not, the whizz of an arrow past me was reality enough.

A wandering band of the Orgs were stalking us! At the whizz of the arrow I made a dash sidewise. My gun was gone; I jerked out my knife. Ama was up, and another arrow barely missed her—an arrow that came from a totally different direction so that I knew we must be already surrounded.

"Ama—lie down! Down—"

A woman under some circumstances can be a terrible handicap. She didn't drop to the ground; she stood gazing around her in terror, and then she came running at me, clutching me so that I was futilely struggling to cast her off. Another arrow sang past our heads, and then from several directions, the Orgs were bursting into the glade.

I tore loose from Ama, but it was no use. Whatever effective fight I might have put up, it could have brought a rain of arrows which might, probably would, have killed the girl.

"Quiet," I murmured. "They've got us. No chance to fight."

I stood trying to shield her as in the dimness the Orgs crowded around us. Ten or more of them, jabbering at us, seizing me and presently shoving us off through the forest.

Two or three others seemed to join us in a moment; and abruptly Ama gasped:

"Tahg! There is Tahg—"

The renegade Senza, quite obviously a leader here, shoved past his jabbering, triumphant men and confronted us. He was seemingly startled, and then triumphant at seeing Ama here. Then his gaze swept to me. He was a big, muscular, but slender fellow. He was clad in a brief brown drape; but his aspect was wholly different from the heavy, misshapen, clumsy-looking Orgs. His thick dark hair fell longish about his ears, framing his hawk-nosed, thin-lipped face. And his narrow dark eyes squinted at me as he frowned.

"Well," he said, "Earthman? New one?" His English was evidently less fluent than Ama's, but it was understandable enough.

"Yes," I agreed. "Friendly—like all Earthmen."

He had signaled to the Orgs, and two of them had shuffled forward and taken Ama from me.

"Jus' good time," Tahg said ironically. "Org gods pleased tonight to have Earthmen—"

Earthmen! The plural! I had little opportunity to ponder it. Roughly I was shoved onward through the forest, back to where it thinned into a stretch of metal desert—and beyond that into a new terrain of stunted, gnarled trees and rope vines on a rocky ground. To me it was an exhausting march. Ama, with Tahg beside her, usually was behind me. Once we stopped and food and water were given me. When we started again, I saw that, at Tahg's direction, one of the savages had hoisted Ama to his back, carrying her in a rope-vine sling. Occasionally other small bands of Orgs joined us, until there were fifty or more of them, triumphantly returning to their village. Their torches were burning now, and a little ahead of us a pack of the huge green-grey mimes were leaping.

Then Tahg came toward me. "Good-bye," he said. "You look more good to me when I see you next time. The gods prepare you now."

* * * *

He turned and was lost in the darkness. My ankles had been fettered with a two-foot length of rope; my wrists were crossed and lashed behind me. No one was with me now but my two captors who urged me forward, impatient at my little jerky steps. The village and its jabbering turmoil and lights was in a moment hidden by a rise of the rocky ground. Then I saw before me a fairly large, square building of stone, flat-roofed, with a cone-shaped stone-pile on top like a crude church spire.

An Org temple. It was windowless; some twenty feet high from ground to its roof. A narrow, rectangular slit of doorway was in front, where two huge torches, like braziers one on either side, were burning. An Org stood between them, with the torchlight painting him— an aged savage in a long, white skin drape which was fantastically ornamented. He was thin and bent, his round brown skull almost hairless, his body shriveled, parched with age. His skinny arms were upraised, outstretched to welcome me.

But my startled gaze turned from him, for on the ground just at the edge of the swaying torchlight, I saw that two figures were lying. Two men, roped and tied into inert bundles.

They were Jan and Torrence!

CHAPTER V

There was a time when, roped and tied like Jan and Torrence, I was laid beside them while in the torchlight, alone with his pagan gods, the ancient Org priest stood intoning his prayers and incantations. It was then that Jan was able to tell me what had happened to him. He was lying between Torrence and me. I had little chance to talk to Torrence. Nor any great desire, for I considered him then merely a craven fellow who had deserted us at the very first of the weird attacks.

Human emotions work strangely. It was obvious now, as we lay there in the darkness, with the aged savage in the torchlight near us—obvious enough that we were doomed to something horrible which at best would end in our death. Yet Jan and I—each having considered the other dead—were for a brief time at least, pleased that we were here. No one yet alive, can normally quite give up hope of escaping death. I recall that in the darkness I was furtively trying to loosen my bonds, twisting and squirming.

"You needn't bother," Torrence muttered. "I've tried all that. And those two damned Orgs who carried you here—they're still watching us."

"Going to take us inside, I guess," Jan whispered. "Inside this temple to—to—"

His shuddering imagination supplied no words. But his idea was right, for presently the old priest was finished with his incantations. His cracked voice called a command and the two savages who had brought me here came from nearby. One by one, they picked us up and carried us inside.

I was the last to go in. The place was a single stone square room. It was lurid with a swaying torchlight. Carved gargoyle images, crude and hideously ugly—grotesque personification of the pagan Vulcan gods—where ranged along the walls. The old priest was standing now on a little dais, between the two interior torches. His arms were upraised toward me as I was carried in; behind him there was a quick stone altar, with a line of smaller images on it. His voice rose, quavering, as I was slowly carried past him; and his hands over me might have been purifying me for the coming rite.

In the center of the room, raised some five feet above the floor, there was a broad stone slab, with a big, grinning, pot-bellied stone image mounted up there. Then I saw that the slab had a broad, cradle-like depression in front of the image. Still bound, lying there side by side, with the belly of the huge image projecting partly over them, were Jan and Torrence. And now the two savages hoisted me up and rolled me among them.

The sacrificial altar. Heaven knows, I could not miss the realization now. There was a weird, acrid, nauseous smell clinging here from former ceremonies. And as I was hoisted up, I saw that the smooth sides of the altar were seared, blackened by the heat of flames which so many times before must have been here.

And the heat—the fire? Within a moment after I was rolled into the saucer-like depression of the alter—with Torrence muttering despairing curses and Jan pallid and grim beside me—outside the temple there sounded a weird gibbering chorus of baying. Ghastly, familiar sound! The mimes—the giant fire-males! Released at the temple doorway, they came bounding in—blobs of leaping red-green flame! A dozen or more of the weird creatures, all of these much larger than the male Jan had killed near the Roberts' spaceship. Fire-males trained for this ceremony. Enveloped in their lurid flames they rushed at the altar, circling it, swiftly running one behind the other so that we were encircled with a ring of leaping flames.

I heard Torrence mutter, "To roast us! Just to roast us slowly—"

* * * *

The shoulders and heads of the running, circling fire-mimes were nearly as high as the altar slab on which we were lying. The flames of them swirled two or three feet higher—blobs of fire which merged one with the other. A circular curtain of mounting flame walling us in. Through it the temple interior was blurred, distorted. Vaguely the figure of the aged priest was visible. He was now on his knees, turned partly away from us as he faced his little row of god-images, supplicating them.

Curtain of swirling fire. Within a moment the heat of it was searing us. Heat slowly intensifying. It was bearable now; but the confined circle of air here was mounting in temperature; the big gargoyle image over us, the metallic-rock slab beneath us both were slowly heating. The smoke and the swirling gas-fumes would choke us into unconsciousness very quickly, I knew. And then the mounting heat would at last make this a sizzling griddle, on which we would lie, slowly roasting....

A chaos of confused phantasmagoria blurred my mind in those first horrible moments.... I saw the old priest, so solemnly, humbly supplicating his gods as he officiated at this gruesome pagan ceremony ... then I could envisage us being carried off, back to the Org village where the people, not worthy of being here in the sacred temple, were so eagerly awaiting us ... then the orgy—sacred feast, endowing its participants with what future virtues and panaceas they conceived their gods would give them....

The end, for us.... Already Jan was pitifully coughing.... But what was this? I felt a shape stir beside me; a small, slender figure with dangling hair; I felt trembling fingers fumbling at my bonds.

Ama! She had crept from a little recess under the giant bulging statue of the gargoyle god, here on the altar. Ama, who had found a chance to slip away from the wooing Tahg, and had preceded us here—hiding up here so that she might try and release us....

But it was too late now. So obviously too late! She had accomplished nothing, save to immolate herself here with us!

Into my ear her terrified voice was whispering, "I thought that the fire-males would not come so soon."

In the blurring, blasting heat and smoke, she had untied us, but of what use? "No—no chance to try and jump," she stammered. "As we fell they would leap upon us—kill us in a moment—"

The sizzling, crackling of the flames—the gibbering baying of the fire-mimes mingling with the incantations of the old priest—it was all a blurred chaos.... Then suddenly I was aware that Jan, coughing, choking, had struggled half erect on the slab. There was just an instant when I saw his contorted face, painted lurid by the flames. Wild despairing desperation was stamped there. But there was something else. An exaltation....

"You—run—" he gasped.

And then he jumped. A wild, desperate leap, upward and out-ward.... It carried him through the curtain of flame and out some ten feet to the temple floor. The thud of his crashing body mingled with the gibbering yelps of the fire-mimes as they whirled and pounced upon him—all of them in a second, merged into a great blob of flame out there on the temple floor where they fought, scrambling over him, ripping—tearing—

Gruesome horror.... I knew in that second that already Jan was dead.... And then I was aware that the other side of the altar, behind the gargoyle image, was momentarily completely dark. All the flam-ing creatures were fighting over Jan's body. Torrence, too, had real-ized it. I saw him stagger up and jump into the darkness. I shoved at Ama; rolled and tumbled her off the slab. We fell in a heap and scrambled erect. The pawing, snarling group of fire-mimes, twenty feet away with the big altar slab intervening, intent upon their scat-tering fragments, for that moment did not heed us. On his little dais by the wall, the old priest had turned and was standing numbed, con-fused. There was no one else in the sacred temple. The single door-way was a vertical slit of darkness. Already Torrence was running for it. I clutched at Ama and we ran.

* * * *

Out into the rocky blackness. I recall that I had the wits to turn us away from where the Org village lay nearby, behind the hillock.... Then, suddenly, from behind a crag, a dark figure rose up. Tahg! Tahg, who had been crouching here, evidently impatient for his feast so that he would be the first to see us as we were brought from the temple....

He stood gasping, startled; and in that same second I was upon him, my fist crashing into his face so that he went backward and down. With desperate haste I caught up a rock from the ground—pounded it on his head—wildly pounding until his skull smashed.... Then I was up, clutching Ama. Torrence already was ten or twenty feet ahead of us in the darkness. We ran after him; he heard us com-ing and waited.

"Which way?" he gasped. "She ought to know. Our spaceship—that would be best—"

At the door of the temple the old priest now was standing screaming. From behind the little hill, answering shouts were responding....

"Is it closer to your village, or to our ship?" I demanded of Ama.

"Why—why to your ship, I think."

"You know the way?"

"Yes—yes, I think so. Not to where you landed—that I do not know. But to the Roberts' ship—"

And the Orgs doubtless would consider that we would head into the Senza country. The forests in that direction would be full of roaming Orgs hunting us....

She and I and Torrence ran, plunging wildly forward in the rocky darkness, with the lights and the turmoil behind us presently fading away into the heavy blank silence of the Vulcan night....

* * * *

I think that there is little I need add. It was a long, arduous journey, but we reached our little spaceship safely. And in a moment, with the rocket-streams shoving downward and with the lower-hull gravity plates in neutral, slowly we were rising into the cloudy darkness.

"You will take me to my people?" Ama said anxiously. "You did promise me—"

"Yes, of course, Ama—we'll land you near your village—"

Queerly enough, it was not until that moment after all the tumultuous events which had engulfed us, that suddenly I remembered the deposits of *allurite* which we had hoped to locate upon Vulcan. If I could take back samples of the ore—to my sponsors that doubtless would be considered the major success—the only success indeed—of my expedition.... It occurred to me then that we could land at the Senza village, and for a little time, prospect from there....

But even that plan was doomed to frustration. I mentioned it to Torrence. "We should head for Earth," he said dogmatically. "I have had enough of this."

It was then, before we had gone far toward the Senza country, that I noticed the rocket streams were acting queerly. A seeming lack of power.... Torrence had gone down into the hull; he came back presently to the turret.

"The Pelletier rotators are slowing," I said. "What's the matter?"

He shook his head. "I noticed it," he said. "Haven't found out yet. You want to come and look?"

I locked the controls, left Ama and went down into the hull with Torrence. In the dim mechanism cubby, as I bent over the Pelletier mechanisms, suddenly Torrence leaped on me! It came as quickly, unexpectedly as that. The culmination of his brooding, murderous, cowardly plans. His heavy face was contorted, his eyes blazing. In his hand he held a sliver of metal arrow. It was bent, doubled over, so that all this time he had been able to keep it hidden in his clothes. The arrow he had taken from Roberts' body, as it lay there near the bow of the wrecked spaceship! The little light in the mechanism cubby gleamed on it now; glistened on the green and red spots of the sleek, sand-colored metal. *Allurite!* The precious substance—not an alloy, not a low-grade *allurium* ore, but *allurite* in its pure state! On Earth this single bent little arrow could be worth a fortune!

And the frenzied Torrence was gloating: "See it, you damn fool—your *allurite*—right under your nose all the time! And now it's mine—" In that second he would have plunged the needle-sharp arrow-point like a stilletto into my heart. But his own frenzied, murderous hysteria defeated him. My fist struck his wrist, knocked his stab-thrust away, with the arrow clattering to the floor. And then I had him by the throat, strangling him until he yielded and I tied him up....

As you who read this, of course, already know from the news reports, I dropped Ama near the edge of the Senza village. I recall now how she stood in the Vulcan night, in the torchlight with the excited crowd of her people behind her; the last I saw of Vulcan was the little figure of her waving at me as I rose into the leaden sky and headed back for Earth.... Maybe—just maybe—I'll return someday to that land where Jan gave his life that his friends might live.

SPACE-FLIGHT OF TERROR

CHAPTER I

The Beginning

IT WAS about nine o'clock, that summer evening—June 10, 2050 A. D.—when Chief Greer called me on split-wave code audiphone.

"Jon Allen? Oh, you Jon—fly down to me at once. I'm in my office—Interplanetary Patrol Building—top floor X-120, under the observatory."

"What's in the air, Chief?" I demanded.

"I'm booking you as a passenger on the *Stardust*. You take off for Mars at midnight. Get down here fast. You haven't much time."

I am Jon Allen, Junior Operative, Shadow Squad Division of the Interplanetary Patrol. My job is undercover work on anything concerning Interplanetary illegality. Sometimes it's trivial, routine stuff; but by the tense urgency now in the Chief's voice, this didn't seem so.

I flew down to mid-Manhattan in my small air-roller; landed on the roof of the towering IP Building. Greer was in his office, alone at his desk with his banks of instruments around him. He waved me to a seat before him. The padded, circular little office was dim with tube-light from a hooded cylinder on the desk. Starlight filtered down from the observatory overhead.

As I entered, Greer signaled for silence. The door slid closed upon us; the trap to the observatory cut off the starlight and the voices of the IP men on duty up there. Then he pressed another lever. The metal walls of the little cubby here crackled for an instant as the sound-absorbing barrage went into them. We were secure against any possible electric eavesdropping.

"As secret as that?" I murmured. My voice was dead, toneless, with the barrage gripping it. "All right. Let's have it."

"A secret shipment of Radiumite-27[1]," he responded.

"Valuable stuff," I murmured. "And I'm to guard it?"

I stiffened. He saw it, and he smiled. "I know what you're think-ing, Jon. About your father—that mystery of his disappearance—"

My father, twenty years ago when I was only four years old, had been a member of the New York Shadow Squad. He had been on the job, guarding a very considerable treasure. The treasure had dis-appeared, and my father with it. Nothing had been heard from him again. It had broken my mother's heart; and she had died a few years later.... Like father; like son. It had put a cloud always upon me. I had no proof of my father's guilt—in my heart I could not believe him guilty.

But now, guarding this shipment of Concentrate-27—suppose something went wrong? Surely this was one case on which I would have to make good!

"You're the only operative I have available," Chief Greer was saying. "And I know I can trust you, Jon." His gesture seemed trying to wave it away. "This Concentrate-27 is damn potent stuff—used to stimulate radioactivity in the baser, commercial ores of radium. Only our Earth-Government can produce it. For war purposes is can be made to incite, in certain uranium alloys a diabolic explosive force—"

"And now we're sending some of it to Mars?" I said. "What in the devil—"

His gesture checked me. "The wisdom of that isn't for us to de-cide. Besides being the basis for the most powerful explosives so far discovered, it has become a big factor in medical radiotherapy."

"I've heard about that."

"The cheapest and best germ-killer yet discovered," he said. "So our medical profession has been secretly using it. And they got per-mission to allow the Martian Human Welfare Society to try it. Natu-rally our Government couldn't refuse that."

"I get your point." Ironic, this stuff that could both kill people and save their lives!

---

1   Radiumite-27—the technical name of a product known only to govern-ment officials and the medical profession. An ultra-radiumite concentration, which in 2048 was discovered and was now being produced by secret formula in the Earth-Federation Government Laboratories. Rumors of it had gotten out, but the details were withheld from the public.

"So now we have sold a small quantity to the Martian Human Welfare Society, for medical use only," Greer went on. "Fair enough. Not much danger that the Martian Government will confiscate it, and turn it into explosives. We'd find that out and it would precipitate war."

"They might use that as a sample, and try and make themselves more," I suggested.

He shook his head. "Can't be done. That's been demonstrated. But the point is, there's enough of the stuff in this shipment to make a lot of explosives. Subversive elements in Mars—plenty of them in Ferrok Shahn, working to overthrow the government—"

"And plenty here on earth," I commented.

"Exactly. They'd pay big to get hold of this shipment. Enough to tempt any band of criminals."

"And you think that news of the *Stardust* carrying it on tonight's flight may have leaked out?"

He shrugged. "That's what we don't know. I could imagine, if any criminals got hold of it, they could sell it on Mars for a thousand decimars. Maybe more. That's ten million platinum-dollars of Earth-currency. A lot of money." Greer smiled wryly as he added, "You could bribe even a pretty honest man with that much money."

I agreed with him there. "In what form is this shipment?"

"A small, leaden-insulated, double-shelled pressure cylinder. The whole thing isn't much bigger than your hand. It will be in the Purser's safe. He and the Captain are the only ones—" Again Greer smiled wryly. "So far as we know, the only ones who are aware it will be there. Or even be on the ship, for that matter."

"Does the Purser know about me?"

Greer shook his head. "Only Captain Allaire knows you. You can have a talk with him, but be damn careful. My idea, having you among the passengers—if there is any undercover stuff going on, you'll have a chance to spot it."

We talked a while more. "Have you ever heard of an Earth-criminal known as 2Y-X-4-4?" Greer demanded abruptly. "He was before your time."

I HAD heard of him. For quite a few years, up to six or seven years ago, he had raised the devil both in Great-New York and Great-London. And he had never been caught. His nickname was Trigger Joe—handy fellow with a gun.

"Practically nothing known about him," Greer was saying, "except the scent of him. The olfactory classifiers got scent of him several times—the bloodhound machine, as the newscasters call it. 2Y-X-4-4—that's his olfactory classification."

The smell of him, so to speak—the inherent scent, different in every human, so that a dog has no trouble in distinguishing them.

"You think he may have something to do with this shipment of Concentrate-27?" I demanded.

Greer hesitated. "He's been inactive all these years. But there's one queer thing—you get suspicious of everything, Jon, in an affair like this—did you ever hear of one Dolly De Vere?"

I had indeed, but I saw no use in going into it with the Chief. I knew her well; was considerably more than half in love with her, to be exact.

"She's a young actress," Greer was saying. "Not a very important one—done television and stage work here in New York, and in Great-London. Just by chance I came upon a bit of stray information. Her father, years ago, was a good friend of this Trigger Joe. It wouldn't incriminate her, of course—she was just a child then."

Dolly De Vere possibly mixed up in this thing! I held myself tense. "And so what?" I murmured.

"Well, she's booked as a passenger on the *Stardust* tonight, and she doesn't seem to have any particular reason for going to Mars."

Dolly going to Mars! I had been out with her as recently as two nights ago, and she had said nothing to me about it!

I left Greer half an hour later. I had already packed and had my luggage sent to the *Stardust*. The little commercial space-liner was taking off from the Staten Island stage of Earth-Mars Spaceways.

Outside the IP Building a public taxi-roller came at me. I took it. Thousands of people work in the giant IP Building who have no connection with Interplanetary Patrol. I was not incautious, being seen coming out of there.

The taxi-roller sped up to a take-off ramp and within a minute we were in the air. I'm not psychic. I had no suspicion of that public-pilot, flying me now to the *Stardust*. To this day I have no idea whether the accident was normal or not. But at all events we went suddenly dead in the air; came down with an emergency landing on a dark ramp near the Staten shorefront.

My driver got out to putter with his mechanisms. "Sorry Chief," he muttered. "How much time we got? The *Stardust* rack ain't so far from here anyway."

"Right," I agreed. "Here's your money. I'll walk it. Take your time fixing whatever's the matter."

IT WAS a dilapidated waterfront; fallen into neglect for many years. Abandoned docks for surface ships; ramshackle old sheds, with almost lightless corridors between them. By night now it was a shadowy shambles. But I had no luggage with me; and a quarter of a mile ahead I could see the glow of tubelights where the *Stardust* was racked, with a bustle of activity around it.

I started off, with the taxi-roller pilot staring after me. I was in a corridor between two big broken sheds when suddenly the signal disc on my chest under my shirt began to heat. A call from Greer! His wave-length heating my disc. I put the tiny plugs in my ears. A police image-lens was mounted on a street pole here; Greer, worried over me, had picked me up through it.

"You're being followed!" Greer's microphonic voice whispered tensely. "Dammit man, get out of there!"

I didn't stop to answer him, ducked into a broken old warehouse, went through it on the run and into another street, almost as dark as the one I had left. A light-pole at a corner had another of the police image-lenses mounted up by the light. Greer picked up the image of me through it.

"Okay," his voice said. "Man in a black cloak—didn't see where he went. Keep going. Goodbye, Jon—good luck."

That figure in the black cloak evidently didn't try to follow me through the warehouse, but he certainly made speed. I shied around the street-light, with a lighted intersection where traffic was passing no more that a hundred yards ahead of me. And suddenly, from off to my left, there was a hiss; a violet stab of heat-bolt. It missed me, but I melted down as though it had drilled me. There was an instant of blank silence. I was lying prone, with my Banning gun cocked up on one elbow. And then I saw the dark-robed figure coming from a shadow! A man, robed and hooded. Fifty feet away.

I'd have drilled him in another second or two; but some fool city-desk policeman must have spotted the bolt-flash through one of these image-posts. He set off an actinic alarm flare. It was over by the traffic intersection—glare of white light which had me just on its fringe.

My Banning gun stabbed its bolt. But too late. The black figure, startled by the glare, had jumped back. I missed him. It was by inches; and the violet heat-beam must have singed the waving bottom of his voluminous cloak. I saw it shrivel and glow for a second as the fabric charred. No time for me to stab again. He was running; within a second he had ducked behind an intervening building and was gone.

The damned actinic glare, and an alarm siren now, was bringing chaos to the neighborhood. The last thing I wanted was to get caught in any turmoil of local-police activity! I got out of there in a hurry; joined a milling pedestrian crowd which was trying to find out what had happened.

So already my connection with this case was known! I had been picked up by someone who was watching Greer's office!

A few minutes later I was on the *Stardust.* For fifteen minutes or so I stood on the little flyer's forepeak, watching the passengers and luggage come aboard—no more than a dozen passengers, this flight; Earth people, a few Martians—a Lunite or two.

Then presently the bulls-eye and the glassite dome-port were sealed. The little *Stardust* lifted. With rocket-tail for atmospheric flight streaming out behind her, she slanted up into the starlight through the stratosphere, with the rocket-engines off and the gravity plates in Earth-repulsion.

Then we were in Interplanetary space. The voyage of terror had begun.

CHAPTER II

Quarry of the Bloodhound Machine

"WHY DIDN'T you tell me you were going to Mars?" I demanded. "See here, Dolly—"

Her eyes avoided me. She was a little beauty, this Dolly De Vere. The starlight, as we sat now on the forepeak of the ship, came down through the overhead glassite pressure-dome and bathed her with its shimmering light.

"I could ask you that same thing, Jon—" she murmured. "And you're not traveling as an IP man are you?"

It was almost as though we were antagonists! A different Dolly, here now on the little *Stardust,* from the girl I had known in New York.

"I won't say anything about your identity, Jon," she added sweetly. "Not unless you insist."

A threat! The *Stardust* was now a day out from the earth. Dolly quite obviously had been avoiding me; it was the first opportunity I had had of being alone with her. Destined to be brief, for two men now came strolling along the deck. One of the passengers, and the ship's Purser. They joined us at once. Dolly had always been a magnet to men.

I gave no hint now that I knew her, and my warning glance suggested that she do the same. She did; but it was as though she was holding a threat over me!

"Interesting profession, theatrical work," the passenger who had joined us presently said, when Dolly told him that she was an actress. His name was J. Tarkington Mantell. He was a big, handsome man. Fifty perhaps. Exceedingly distinguished-looking, with a great shaggy mass of gray-white hair.

"You were an actor?" Dolly Marks asked him.

"Some years ago," he smiled. "Mantell the Magician. Surely you have heard of the great scientific illusions of Mantell the Magician?" He chuckled. "The public loves to be fooled. It is marvelous, what you can do with science, Miss De Vere, to make things seem what they are not."

He was a likable fellow, this J. Tarkington Mantell. He had retired now from the stage and television. For half an hour he regaled us reminiscences of his big stage illusions, where with intricate mechanical trappings and a skilled application of modern science he had fooled his gullible public.

"Do something for us now," Dolly said.

"Oh no, he laughed. "You would see through me. One needs soft lights, and music. I would be humiliated." He winked at me. "I would get caught in my trickery. You are in the profession, Miss De Vere. Tell us about yourself."

I sat tense, listening to her explain that she was traveling to Mars to fill a theatrical engagement in Ferrok-Shahn. It sounded plausible enough to these others. But not to me—for why hadn't she mentioned it when I had seen her so short a time ago? Leaving for Mars, without saying goodbye to me! Was she really connected now with this Trigger Joe? And was he involved in some plot now against the Cylinder of Concentrate-27?

I could hardly believe it. Dolly was only seventeen—small, dark, with snappy dark eyes and pert red lips. A girl of brains, without question. Self-reliant from having earned her living on the stage for several years. And I had thought I had known her so well!

THE CONVERSATION went on. I said very little. Somehow a queer uneasy tenseness was on me. That shadow that the mystery of my father had cast upon me always seemed so much greater now with the importance of this affair. I sat watching Dolly, the Purser and Mantell—alertly watching, suspicious of everyone and everything.

"My first space-flight," Dolly was saying. Her gaze drifted off to the glittering stars through the pressure-dome. "It's even more beautiful than I had imagined."

The *Stardust's* Purser—a stocky fellow with close-clipped black hair that bristled over his forehead like a wire-brush—was sitting with us. His name was P. B. Franklin.

"I hope we have a pleasant voyage," he commented. "But our crew doesn't seem to think so."

"What's that mean?" Mantell demanded. His sleek graceful hand brushed his crop of iron-gray hair with a gesture. "Trouble with the crew? For a fact, I heard one of those Martian fellows muttering to himself, back on the stern deck a while ago. I wondered—"

"Accursedly superstitious, these deckhand minions," Franklin said wryly. "All nonsense, of course. But they're saying this is a voyage of doom, this trip. Ten of them, and they're all alike. We're star-crossed, this voyage—that's what they're saying. Astrologically, the stars were bad, for us to start last midnight. There was an electric aura around the moon, just as we took off. And a meteorite crossed our bow, just as we went into the stratosphere. Stuff like that.… Oh, do I frighten you, Miss De Vere? Why, I'm sorry."

I had been watching her. Terror had leaped into her eyes. Terror that seemed out of all proportion to the Purser's words. And yet certainly I could feel it myself. Queer undercurrent of horror that was running over the ship. As though everyone on board seemed to sense an undercurrent of mystery, this voyage. Ship of doom. There is nothing so communicable as fear. I am a hard-boiled fellow, an IP man has to be. But still I could feel that queer clutching inside of me—the thought that there was something grew-some here—something not to be understood, nor translated into terms of rational science. No wonder the superstitious crew was frightened!

"Sorry if I've alarmed you," the Purser said again.

"Why no," she murmured. She tried to smile. "That's—very interesting, Mr. Franklin. Silly superstitions—"

The stocky, red-faced Purser looked contrite. "Of course it's all nonsense," he declared. "We're destined to have a perfect voyage. No chance for a space-storm. The sun-spots are normal this month. Captain Allaire checked every cosmic condition carefully before we took off. That sort of thing is never made public, Miss De Vere, but you can be assured we don't overlook it. The electronic space-pressures, all the way from here to Mars, are perfectly normal. Nothing can happen to us—"

"Well let's hope not," Mantell commented with his ready smile. Don't let's look for trouble. Imagination is a powerful thing. I used to find that with my audiences. If you could get them imagining things—"

HIS VOICE trailed off. I saw that he was gazing up toward the bow-peak. The bow lookout was there at his little electro-telescope. And near him were two big Martian deckhands. Brown, burly fellows, clad in rough Earth-garb of short jacket and wide flopping trousers. I could see that they weren't natives of the Martian Union—far too burly—and too tall, nearly seven feet. They were standing together. They seemed to be whispering as they gazed at us.

I leaned toward Mantell. "Those Martians up there," I murmured. "Watching us—"

Franklin the Purser heard me. "New members of the crew, this voyage. They're the worst with their damned superstitions—"

New members! Martians, from the Dark Country outside the Martian Union. That was the region full of revolutionary plotters against the Martian Government! Leaders of subversive activities there certainly would pay big for that little leaden cylinder of Concentrate-27, which I knew was now locked in Purser Franklin's safe, in his office-cubby here no more than a hundred feet from us!

Then suddenly, from the side deck between the cabin-superstructure and the side wall of the pressure-dome, a man came slouching. Another member of the crew—a little Earthman. He was muttering to himself, and his face was chalk-white.

As he came past us, the Purser hailed him. "You Jones—what the devil's the matter with you?"

He stared at us. "I seen it," he muttered. "An hour ago—I seen it in one of the cabin corridors—"

"Seen what?" the Purser demanded.

"There's a ghost on this ship, Mr. Franklin. That's what they're all sayin' an' I've seen it. A dead thing, but it won't stay dead—"

Beside me I heard Dolly Marks suck in her breath with a little suppressed cry. Whatever terror she had shown before was nothing to that stamped on her face now. My hand went out and touched her arm.

"Take it easy," I murmured.

Mantell was blankly staring at the terrified deckhand. Franklin demanded: "What do you mean, a ghost on this ship?"

"A dead man's head," Jones chattered. "I seen it. His head— somebody must have cut his head off when he got killed. An' now his head won't stay dead. It floats. I seen it—a big purple head, all glowin' like light—Oh my Gawd, there it is now!" He ended with a squeal of terror as he stared up to the dome over our heads.

I was aware, in that stricken second, that there was a faint humming crackle quite near me. Mantell must have heard it also, for he stared at me with a look of startled astonishment. A little crackle down on the deck near us. But the thought of it was stricken away as we started, following the deckhand's frightened gesture.

The ghost of a dead man's head! It was about that big—a luminous round purple thing. Up in the starlight, under the pressure-dome thirty feet over us, it suddenly had appeared. For a second it hung in midair above the peak of the little control turret. And then it moved, floating….

"Oh my Gawd, it's comin' down at us!" Jones squealed.

Slowly it was floating down. Crackling, with a faint humming hiss. I think we were all out of our chairs, standing clutching at each other. Another second or two. Was there the goggling face of a dead man, visible in the front of that floating ghost-head? For just a split-second my excited imagination made me think so. The damned thing seemed almost as though it would lunge at us. But ten feet away it turned, hung for a second on the yard-arm of the little electric cargo-loader here on the fore-deck. And then it was fading. A purple wraith. It quivered and was gone.

"Well, I'll be damned," Mantell muttered.

Jones had darted away from us in terror. The Martians in the bow were staring; then they ran down into the hold-companionway.

"Well—" Franklin gasped. "Well—"

I recovered my wits. We stared around us in the dim starlight. There was nothing here now. "That was a ball of ionized air," I said.

IONIZED air? Was it really that? St. Elmo's Fire, as the sailors of the old surface ships used to call it. Purple balls that would hang on the ship's rigging during thunderstorms. But what was a ball of ionized air doing here inside the *Stardust?* There was no electrical disturbance here.

"You had the right idea," Mantell said to me softly a few moments later. Dolly had gone to her sleeping cubby. The Purser had dashed away with John Thomas, the ship's young First Officer to try and restore order among the crew and passengers.

Mantell had drawn me aside. "That was ionized air, all right." He laughed grimly. "I ought to know—I've produced balls of light-fire like that in my theatrical illusions. Never was able to make them seem to look like the ghost of a human head—"

"That was imagination," I said. "I realized that as I stared at it—"

He nodded. "Those damned things even can be directed," he asserted. "Radio-pressure control—make them travel in a directed course—"

But who was creating this horror on the *Stardust?* And Why? Again I wondered if Trigger Joe, with his olfactory classification of 2Y-X-4-4 could be on board. I had a small model of the bloodhound machine with me—no bigger than my palm. Furtively I had tried it, with its effective range of only a few feet, upon each of these men I had met. But always the action was negative.

"Well, guess I'll go into the Smoking Lounge and see if I can rake up a game of cards," Mantell said. He flashed me his likable smile, but it was lugubrious. "Whatever's going on here, I don't want to let it get me."

I left him at the Lounge door. By ship's routine it was now nearly midnight. I went to my room, midway down one of the small super-structure corridors. It was lightless. My door was locked. The single small window which opened to the side deck was a faint rectangle of starlight that filtered through the outside pressure-wall.

I sat on my bed, pondering. Space-flight of doom. But this horror was being created. The ship's crew terrorized. Why? So that the criminal could go ahead with his plans, under cover of this terror?

I had never felt less like sleep. In the pallid darkness I sat listening to the faint throb of the ship—the hum of the air-renewers, the ventilating system; and the faint rhythmic oscillation of the pressure-absorbing Erentz-current[2] in the double-shelled hull-walls and the big glassite dome which arched over the decks and the superstructure roof. Now, so late, the few passengers doubtless had gone to bed. I knew there would be two or three members of the crew on duty; Captain Allaire at the controls in the little forward turret; and Controlman Roberts down in his mechanism cubby in the vessel's hull.

Upon impulse I decided to go up and talk to Captain Allaire. I had had no opportunity yet to be alone with him; he had flashed me a significant look of recognition as I came aboard, but that was all. I went quietly out; closed my cubby door. The narrow vaulted corridor which vertically bisected the forty foot long cabin superstructure, was dim and silent. The passengers' doors, each with a glowing nameplate of its occupant, were all closed.

---

2   Erentz-current: a swift oscillation of current which by its kinetic energy absorbs the latent pressure-energy of the *outer* shell of the double wall. Thus, that pressure, absorbed into the swiftly oscillating current, cannot reach the inner shell of the hull and dome. Perfected by Erentz, Earth-scientists in 2010, making space-flight possible.

Silently I went forward, to where the corridor emerged at the bowpeak deck triangle, where we had been sitting earlier in the evening. No one was there, except the forward lookout at the extreme bow-peak, seated at his telescope. The stars beyond our bow—great blazing gems in a black firmament—glittered with celestial glory. Red Mars was there, still small, shining, dull-red disc.

At the corner of the superstructure I passed Purser Franklin's office, with a grating closing its entrance. The door to his sleeping cubby was open. He was not there. By his dim night-light the big electric-sealed safe was visible, closed and locked upon its secret treasure.

A light down the side deck attracted me—an opened doorway from which blue tubelight radiance was streaming out. I knew it was the men's smoking lounge. The murmur of voices was audible. I went to where, without being seen on the shadowed deck, I could see the lounge interior. It was blue with smoke of tobacco arrant-cylinders. The card-game was in progress, with gold-leaf stakes. Mantell and two other men passengers, playing with one Jenks—a gold-leaf professional gambler. I knew little Willie Jenks by reputation—rat-faced, glib little fellow, card-sharper, skilled with the trickery of his fingers at card-manipulation. The stakes evidently weren't high. Jenks was raking in the leaf, much to the amusement of Mantell. As I watched, Mantell let out a roar of laughter.

"Very clever, Jenks. You take me back to my theatrical days. The hand is quicker than the eye. The public likes to be fooled. You should get rich, Jenks."

I moved away. And suddenly I stopped, stricken. Down at the other end of the side-deck, where it emerged to the stern deck-triangle, a blob moved. Dolly! A sheen of light caught upon her dark short skirt—the satin pink-whiteness of her legs.

Which way had she gone? I couldn't tell. I was at the stern triangle in a moment. There was nothing. What was she doing, roaming the vessel at this time of night? Locating where the crew-hands were placed? Finding out who was in the smoking lounge?

Finding out that Purser Franklin was there! *That the safe in his office-cubby was unguarded?*

The thoughts leaped at me; made my heart pound. Was she getting the lay of things so that she could break into the safe?

My padded shoes were soundless as I went forward in the corridor. Franklin's dim cubby back of the grating quite evidently was still unoccupied. No sign of anything here. And then I glimpsed the furtive girl again. This time she was midway of the superstructure, just vanishing into one of the little cross corridors. Had someone preceded her? I got that vague impression, as though I had seen the flick on some garment that wasn't hers.

It was the cross corridor in which the girl's sleeping cubby was located. She had obviously gone into her room when I got there. Her door was closed.

For a moment I hesitated. My electric listener, pressed against the metal panel of the door, yielded only a thumping that might be the girl's footsteps inside her room; her quick, hurried breathing sounding as though she were terrified. But mingled with it there was something else. A blur. The sound of someone else, further away from me, in the room with her?

And then I heard a man's low voice. "Whatever should happen, Dolly, you stay here. Understand?"

"Yes. Oh, but please—"

"Easy—don't raise your voice. You know we can't be seen talking together. Even in here—"

The man's voice suddenly checked itself, dropping so low that I couldn't catch the phrase. And then I heard him preparing to leave her room. Hastily I withdrew down to an angle of the corridor.

Her door opened. A man came out, turned the other way in the corridor. A big man, bent, with wide thin shoulders. His peaked traveling cap was low on his forehead. One of the passengers. I had seen him at other times, but only at a distance. In the blue tubelight of the corridor now, as he turned away from me, I caught a glimpse of the light glinting on his big goggling eyeglasses.

One of the deckhands came along, passing me as I stood at the corridor intersection.

"Who is that fellow?" I demanded.

"Man in A17," the deckhand said. "Old fellow, traveling alone. Keeps to himself pretty much, seems like."

The deckhand passed on. He hadn't seen the goggled man come from Dolly's cubby. I stood for a moment; then I padded to the corridor angle. Just in time to see the goggled man going into A17. The doorlock clicked as he closed it after him.

Within a minute I had padded out to the side deck again and was crouching at the window of A17. It was barred and shrouded, but there was a tiny ventilating slit through which a rift of air was drifting outward. I shoved my Banning gun back into my pocket; brought out my little model of the olfactory classifier. The bloodhound machine. Here, in this room—this goggled old man—was one passenger on whom I had not yet used it. This type portable model was useless except at very close range, and with direct air-current. I had that now, and it might work.

I pressed its tiny power-button. Weird, quivering little machine, snuffing as it sucked in the air while I held it at the window vent. Then its dials were stirring. The scent, coming out the window! I tuned the little receivers. And the verification came. The dial-pointers whirled, quivered and then hovered almost motionless.

2Y-X-4-4! Trigger Joe! The notorious criminal! *He was here!* I had him trapped here in A17!

CHAPTER III

Theft of the Cylinder

CALL this a confession if you like. I started, in that second to try and crack open that barred window. But I didn't. I contemplated going to the Captain with what I had learned. But I didn't do that either. The thought of Dolly—her beauty, her terror, my feelings for her back in New York—the fact that I had thought, back there only a few days ago, that she was falling in love with me—all that rushed over me now.

Trigger Joe had been her father's best friend. He was a wanted man—wanted on both Earth and Mars. But those were old crimes. They did not concern me now. Was he here on the *Stardust* plotting to secure the cylinder of Concentrate-27? I had no proof of that. And if he was, he couldn't escape from the little *Stardust,* out here in the infinite realms of Interplanetary space.

I sat in my cubby, pondering it. Whatever this brewing plot—I knew Trigger Joe's identity now. I would be prepared for whatever move he might make.

I did not undress, but I think I must have dozed. And suddenly the thump of something striking the corridor wall outside my door roused me, brought me to my feet! A crash! And a man's muttered oath of horror!

I rushed out. In the dim empty corridor one of the ship's stewards—a little Earth-man—was crouched against the wall, white-faced, staring down the corridor with a look of terror.

"What the devil happened to you?" I demanded.

"That ghost-head! That purple ball," he muttered. "It went past here jus' now. Nearly hit me—I jumped back."

His startled jump had cracked him against the corridor wall.

"Head of a dead man," he was chattering. "You, sir—you ain't seen it? I guess there's lots of 'em—my Gawd, sir, this one's going all over the ship. It's got everybody frightened—"

I dashed away, following his gesture. A purple ball of ionized air, radio-pressure-controlled? Mantell's warning words came back to me. These accursed balls of light-fire could be directed by some intricate form of remote control.

This one quite evidently was being controlled! It was roaming the ship, bringing terror to everyone who encountered it. I saw the accursed thing within a minute as it floated along one of the corridors—glowing purple ball, the size of my head. A faint hissing hum came from it.

And suddenly it turned into a companion-way where ladder-steps led steeply downward into the *Stardust's* hull! I followed it down. There was a catwalk half way down in the hull, with mechanism rooms opening from it. The ball slowly floated along the catwalk a few feet and then plunged farther downward.

I reached the hull bottom—a narrow passage. Cargo rooms were here. And midway of the ship, I knew, there was a pressure-lock, exit port.[3]

---

3   Pressure lock, standard, though differing in size, for all modern commercial space-ships. A small, sealed air-pressure room, with an inner and an outer doorslide, automatically controlled so that both may not be open at once. For exit, the inner slide is closed. The outer one slowly opens, so that the air in the lock hisses, out into the vacuum of space. For entrance, the process is reversed. The

The purple ball passed the lock entrance. Slowly it was fading now. A wraith, and then it was gone. I came to the pressure lock. Emergency air-pressure suits were racked against the wall in the little lock-chamber. And over in one dark corner there was a blob. It looked like a huge piece of luggage—the luggage of one of the passengers which had been brought here. I went in and examined it.

It was a folded, one-man volplane.[4] Not much more than a power unit. Synthetic food and concentrated water were here with it. The power unit of tiny rocket-stream and gravity plates was charged and ready.

Someone on the *Stardust* was preparing for a getaway! Trigger Joe?

IT TOOK me hardly more than a minute to de-charge the volplane batteries, so that the rocket stream would be inert and the gravity plate useless. The criminal would not notice what I had done—but he would quickly find he couldn't get very far with this apparatus! Once he tried it, he would be caught red-handed!

I got back to the upper side deck, at the side of the superstructure. And abruptly there was a sudden crackle a few feet away from me on the deck. An electric crackle! A hissing! A tiny shower of sparks!

I stared. I could see that it was deranged electricity; and all in that second I could hear it spreading around the ship. Then one of the purple ghost-balls came floating along the deck. It hissed against a bulls-eye port and died. But up at the bow triangle I could see another.

The *Stardust* went into chaos. The lookout was shouting. From up at the turret I heard Captain Allaire's startled oath. And then the little vessel lurched—through the side-dome I could see the starfield shifting as we turned over.

A space-storm! Impossible by meteorological-cosmic forecasts! But it was here. And already the little *Stardust* was in distress! The crackling sizzle of deranged electricity that darted like little lightnings all over the ship's interior, in a moment was gone. But it left

outer slide closes. The inner one, slowly opening, admits the ship's air into the lock.

4   Volplane. Popularly known as "space-sled." Suitable for short trips. A six-foot long sled-like apparatus, usually with a single seat. In effect, merely a power unit, with the occupant wearing the regulation air-pressure space-suit.

fumes. Choking fumes of chlorine and monoxide products. The crew-man on guard at the forepeak was still shouting. Passengers' doors were opening. Alarmed voices. Startled questions. Then I heard one of the crew in the corridor.

"Back in your rooms everybody! Captain's orders. No danger—jus' an outer space-disturbance. We'll be through it in a minute." The deckhand in the corridor dashed up to me. "Can't roam around, sir. Capt'n's orders. Get in your room. Electric disturbance—ventilator dynamos went out, but they're all right now."

"The Captain wants to see me," I muttered. "Don't bother me." I pushed past him.

From his sleeping-cubby door, Mantell came at me. He looked frightened, but he was trying to grin. "Space-storm?" he gasped. "But I thought the Purser said—"

"We evidently ran into one," I told him. "Better stay in your room—guess we're all right now."

That damned excited deckhand was still herding me. I let him shove me down the corridor. Then I got away from him; ran to the side deck. "You—Allen—Jon Allen—"

It was Captain Allaire calling me. He was forward on the deck, starting up a companion ladder. He gestured for me to follow him.

THE Captain's control-turret was a small circular room set upon the forward end of the superstructure roof. It was about ten feet above the forward deck triangle; looked down upon it. Behind the turret, connected with it by an interior door-oval, was the small chart-room. And behind that, there was the open forty foot roof of the superstructure, with the bulging glassite dome covering it with eight feet of headroom.

I dashed up a side ladder and ran the length of the superstructure roof; went into the back door-entrance of the little chart-room.

The Captain was there. He gripped me. "You, Allen," he said softly, "been wanting to see you. Have you overheard any—" He checked himself; we had no barrage to guard against eavesdroppers here.

I put my mouth to his ear. "Plenty to tell you—when we get a chance—"

A deckhand came on the run. "Those two Martians in the crew—can't locate them, sir," he gasped to the Captain.

"What in the devil!" Allaire was a heavy-set, choleric fellow. His fist thumped the chart-room table. "Go find them, bring them up here. I want to know where they got their ideas on this being a voyage of doom. By Heaven, it looks it—"

When we were alone again he swung on me. "Space-storm, Allen. We ran into a supercharged magnetic field, quite evidently. Deranged our interior power for a minute. Must have put the gravity shifting mechanisms out of commission—"

Our suddenly shifted gravity-plates had made the little *Stardust* turn over. The starfield outside was still crazily swinging. Allaire swung me another warning look. Then he buzzed his audio-tube which had direct voice-transmission down to Control-man Roberts in the hull mechanism cubby.

"Roberts! You, Roberts?"

"Yes, Captain—" Roberts' voice came back, muffled through the tube.

"All right now?"

"Yes, sir. Guess so. Deranged electricity. It threw everything out. But Captain—I understood there was no space-storm possible in this—"

Allaire flung me a queer look. "Get the gravity plates shifted back where they were, Roberts," he ordered.

"Yes, sir. The air-purifiers went dead—but I got 'em working now."

Allaire disconnected and swung on me. "Something damn queer about this, Allen," he muttered. "Ever since we left New York—crew been raising hell. Superstitions—ghost-balls of fire."

I leaned over him. "The Purser's safe," I said softly. "We ought to guard it now. All this chaos and terror—a good time for—"

"Good Heavens, yes." He looked startled.

I could see that angle of it now. Someone creating this confusion and terror, and under cover of it getting the cylinder of Concentrate-27. And then making a get-away in that little volplane down there in the pressure-lock.

"You keep your eye on the safe, Allen," Allaire was telling me. And where the devil is Franklin—"

A cry out on the dim, starlit superstructure roof made us whirl. It was Purser Franklin. He came staggering toward us, hair disheveled, face pallid, his braided coat uniform torn and dirty.

"Something—jumped me," he gasped. "Down by my office. Lights went out. Somebody—something knocked me down. Unconscious for a minute—or maybe the damned chlorine fumes—"

We dragged him into the chart-room. I gripped the Captain. "Something I want to tell you—" Surely it was all right for Franklin to realize my identity now—

But my words died in my throat. The Purser stiffened us with his next gasp.

"When I—I came to my senses I saw that the safe was cracked," he was muttering. "Cracked by one of those purple balls! It—it—that cylinder there—it's gone, Captain!"

The cylinder of Concentrate-27! Stolen from under our noses!

CHAPTER IV

Bandit Trapped in Space!

WE WERE all three stricken into a moment of horrified silence. Then I came to my senses. Allaire was gripping the Purser, demanding more details. I left them; rushed down the ladder to the forepeak deck-triangle. The little *Stardust* had steadied now, swinging back onto her course. There was no one in sight except the bow lookout. The air was purer here now. The ventilators, again seemingly working normally, had sucked away the fumes of the free-running electronic radiance.

I ran to the Purser's cubby. Its grating door was ajar; the dim light still burning inside. Banning gun in hand, I went in. The safe was open. As Franklin had said, the cylinder was gone.

On the safe-lock there was a fused, burned area. But it didn't look as though a ball of ionized air had made it. I knew that was hardly possible.

And then I tensed. This fused spot here, hadn't cracked open the safe-lock! The lock was broken now, but it seemed as though it had been done on the inside—after the door was opened. The purple ball that the Purser had seen was a blind! This was a plant, to make us think that the safe had been cracked open. It had not been. It was opened normally, by someone who knew the intricacies of the lock-combination! Had Trigger Joe done it? How had he gotten the information?

My heart was cold as I thought of Dolly. In Heaven's name, how was she mixed up in this thing? An accomplice of Trigger Joe? Or just his victim, forced now to do what he told her?

But of one thing I was sure. My fingers itched to get a grip on that fellow's throat. He was here, somewhere on the *Stardust*. And now he had the treasure-cylinder. His time for a get-away, of course. The ship was in complete turmoil from the space-storm. Would he try now to get away in his volplane?

I ran to A17, to see if he was there. It was closed and locked. My Banning gun, with spreading diffused ray, was a good impromptu heat-torch. I melted the metal doorlock in a moment and burst in.

The dim sleeping cubby was empty. Then I ran to Dolly's room. Its door was unlocked. She wasn't there. Then as I reached the corridor I caught a glimpse of her down near its stern end. And she saw me. She took one look and ducked into a companionway that led down into the hold. I was there in a few seconds. No sign of her. The iron ladder-steps went steeply down. I descended a level; came to the transverse catwalk. The place was dim with shadows; only an occasional spot of tubelight. The narrow catwalk ran from bow to stern. The ship's mechanisms were under it, but to the sides there were several dark little cubbies—storage rooms; mechanism control-rooms of the air-renewers, the rocket-stream engines and pressure-tanks; the ventilating system and the gravity-plate pneumatic shifters.

Where had Dolly gone? She could have ducked into any one of these cubbies. Gun in hand I padded past two or three of them. Light streamed out of a doorway amidships. I knew it was Roberts' main control-room. Perhaps he had seen her.

At his doorway I stood transfixed. He was lying on the floorgrid, ghastly in the blue tubelight, with a knife buried to its hilt in his heart! Something was clutched in his hand. I bent down. It was a bit of charred black fabric. The man in the burned cloak had killed him! The man who had tried to drill me, back in New York!

Then a faint gasped cry out on the dark catwalk made me whirl. Dolly! She stood in the doorway, her face livid, contorted with horror. I jumped and seized her.

"You saw who did that? Stabbed him—"

"No! Oh, my God, no."

I believed her. Certainly she would hardly have had time. I had followed her down here only a few moments ago.

"I—I wanted to tell you something," she gasped.

"So you ran away from me? Damn queer way of trying to tell me something—"

"I was frightened. I thought you might shoot at me."

I STOOD gripping her shoulders. "There was a man in your room a while ago. Where is he?"

Agonized terror swept her face. "No! No," she gasped. "That's a lie. There was no one—"

"Oh, yes, there was! It's you who are lying—" I swear it cut into me, being rough with her. That's queer, too. But there was something weirdly pathetic about her, now more than ever in her terror.

"Oh, please—" she gasped. "There wasn't anyone with me. I swear it."

"You're looking for him now?" I took that shot in the dark, and it seemed to strike home. "That's what you're doing down here, Dolly? Looking for him?"

"No, I tell you!"

"Well, you can see he's a murderer—" I gestured at the ghastly corpse of Roberts. She stared numbly; and then I added, "And you or he got into the Purser's safe. Stole something—"

It certainly wasn't Dolly who had rifled Franklin's safe! The look of blank amazement on her face made that clear. I was dragging her along the catwalk now.

"Where—where are you going with me?" she murmured.

"You had something to tell me?" I demanded.

"Yes. I—he—"

"He?" I echoed.

She tried to correct herself, with a new anguish of terror on her face. "No! I didn't mean that. I mean—I overheard something two of the crew-hands were saying. Two Martians, but they were talking with somebody else. One of the ship's officers, I guess."

Those two Martian deckhands who now had vanished!

We had reached the control turret. Captain Allaire was here alone. He gaped at me, as I came in still gripping the girl.

"You find that—thing we lost?" he demanded.

"No."

"Well, by Heaven," he thundered, "there'll be nobody get away with it. We've got the damned thief here. I'll search the ship—search everybody—"

Suddenly Dolly was murmuring, "That's what I wanted to tell you, John. Those Martians in the crew were saying—somebody's paid them big and he's going to make a get-away, with a cylinder or something. That's why all this confusion has been created—"

Allaire stared at me. "A get-away," he echoed. "Well, there'll be nobody get off my ship, here or in port, until we've searched every damn—"

A cry from the bow lookout interrupted him. And then we all saw it. A little blob out in space, visible through the side bulls-eyes. A blob no more than a hundred feet away from the *Stardust*. The tiny volplane. It hung there in the vacuum of space. Dimly within it we could see the lone seated figure—black-cloaked, black-hooded shape.

Trigger Joe, trying to make his get-away with the cylinder! He was bending down, frantically working at the volplane's controls.

But he wasn't getting anywhere! I had de-charged that power-unit! His rocket-stream wouldn't work! His gravity plates were inert!

BANDIT trapped in space! His tiny volplane and his own body within it—an infinitesimal mass compared to the bulk of the *Stardust*. His initial shove had carried him a hundred feet or so. But now the *Stardust's* gravity pull was drawing him back!

Inexorable forces of nature! He was hanging out there with a side-drift, so that slowly the volplane was finding an orbit of its own—by balancing forces, slowly beginning to circle the ship. Weird little satellite!

"Got him!" Allaire roared. "By Heaven, there he is, with the cylinder. He reached for an audiphone. "We'll have him aboard in a few minutes, Allen! By God, I'll go down there myself and put on a space-suit—"

A shout from down on the forepeak made us turn. John Thomas, our young First Officer was down there. He shouted and started to come up the front ladder. Then from down in the blood-red gloom of the forepeak, a tiny violet bolt stabbed up. Young Thomas screamed a little. There was the sickening smell of burning flesh wafting up to us as for an instant his body hung balanced. Then he crashed back to the forepeak.

Hell broke loose in that second on the little *Stardust.* That shot into Thomas was a signal. Other shots answered it. Shots back at the stern. Screams down in the superstructure. The ship's lights wavered; then went totally dark so that there was nothing but the blood-glare. In the lurid dimness I was gripping Dolly, with an arm about her. And I felt Allaire shoving at me. And heard his voice:

"Why—why Allen—they dare attack us? Close that chart-room door."

He was dragging his weapons out of the rack. Then he dashed across the turret, drew down its metal shades to narrow slits; banged its door. I came back from closing up the chart-room. Down on the forepeak I saw a figure leap upon the bow lookout and stab him. Passengers were screaming now down in the superstructure. An Earth-man and woman came staggering out onto the peak. The same lurking figure leaped at them; sprayed them with a spreading heat beam.

A massacre. No more than ten or twenty seconds had passed. Through the ship's alarm-address system, Allaire had shouted commands for anyone loyal to come to the turret here. But no one could come. My shot stabbed twice down to the forepeak, missed that lurking figure. One of our officers; I caught a glimpse of his braided uniform. The screams in the superstructure, and the shots and sounds of fighting…

AND then I saw that during the murderous chaos the bandits were searching the ship; searching the bodies of the passengers; and we could hear their shouts as they tramped around the superstructure. Searching for the cylinder? That was queer. Why would they do that, when their leader Trigger Joe, out there in space, supposedly had it? We could see him out there now. He had abandoned his efforts to work the volplane. Then suddenly he stood up, jumped from it.

The lunge kicked the volplane farther away. And Trigger Joe's body, grotesque, bloated shape of big puffed air-suit, came wafting in closer to the hull-side. He would get back into the port in a moment; back to join his triumphant conspirators.

"Where in the devil is Franklin?" Allaire was muttering. "Dead by now, probably—"

Then we saw Purser Franklin on the forepeak, where now half a dozen bodies were lying. Allaire shouted at him to come up. But instead, as he saw he was discovered, he jumped behind the dismantled cargo-loader. A bolt from his gun stabbed up at us. It missed the window-slit; struck the metal window-shade with a fountain shower of red, green and yellow sparks.

Franklin, one of the bandits! That made me understand more things. Trigger Joe was working with Franklin! Of course the safe hadn't been broken into! Franklin himself had opened it and taken out the cylinder, with which Trigger Joe had tried to make his get-away. And Franklin would have stayed here and never been suspected.

But still there was a flaw in my reasoning. Why were the bandits searching for the cylinder now?

Trigger Joe was still visible out there in space, near the port.

"So Franklin is one of them?" Allaire was muttering. "And who else?"

We had no way of knowing. A sudden unnatural silence had settled upon the vessel. Charnel ship of death. One thing was sure—whoever was loyal to us now was dead. Captain Allaire and I, embattled here in the turret and chart-room. And Dolly Marks with us. What, in Heaven's name was her real connection with this murderous banditry?

She was crouching now in a corner of the turret, staring at us. I gripped Allaire, told him swiftly about Trigger Joe, the leader of our adversaries. Dolly's eyes stared at me numbly as I spoke. Eyes with anguish in them.

Allaire and I were watching at a turret window. The blood-red forepeak, with its strewn bodies, momentarily showed nothing moving.

"What we call the bloodhound machine, Captain," I was saying. "I used it to spot him in the girl's cubby—" I had the little classifier in my hand as I spoke. And suddenly I gasped. Its dials were still set to pick up the scent-classification 2Y-X-4-4. And now abruptly I saw that they were quivering! They were getting the scent from close range!

2Y-X-4-4 was here, within a few feet of us! That wasn't Trigger Joe out there in space! He was here!

I stared around the dim turret; then dashed into the adjoining chart-room. And then I saw him—a dark blob crouching in a shadowed corner half under the chart-table.

He rose up to jump me as I lunged at him!

CHAPTER V

The Fight in the Turret

BEHIND me in the chart-room, I heard Dolly scream. Her anguished words: "Oh, please— Oh, my God—"

From under the table the blob rose up—a big man, with scraggly sandy hair; a gaunt white face with burning, weird eyes. His goggles were discarded now. My gun stabbed its tiny bolt, but from behind me with another scream, the girl grabbed my elbow. The bolt crackled down against the opposite wall with a fountain-splash of sizzling sparks.

And then I collided with my antagonist. My lowered head struck his chest and he went backward, with me on top of him.

"Oh, please—Oh, don't—don't kill him—" Dolly gasped.

I was aware that Allaire had come running, and was poised with his gun trying to stab a bolt into the man under me. And Dolly was screaming her terrified protest. The fellow was on his back, with me sprawled on him. I felt his skilled fingers clutching my wrist, turning aside my gun. My left fist struck him in his face. Queerly it made him instantly go limp. His head sagged back. Gaunt white face, hollow-cheeked with burning dark eyes. Exceedingly high cheekbones; and hooked nose. His mouth goggled with gasping breath…

Queer. No fight in him. I felt Dolly as she threw herself down upon me, clutching at me frantically. And then I was dimly aware that an outside bolt had struck against the chart-room window. It made the Captain rip out a curse as he ran there, answering the outside shot.

"Oh, please—" the girl was moaning at me. "Don't you see—he can't fight—don't—don't kill him—"

2Y-X-4-4! Trigger Joe. No question of his identity. Notorious wanted man of ten years ago. He was lying here now. No wound seemed on him. But he lay gasping, his mouth, with thin ashen lips, goggled with his labored breath. And Dolly was pleading with me not to kill him.

I slid off him, still sprawled watchfully beside him; and at once the girl flung herself down, with an arm under his head, raising him up, her hand smoothing his forehead where his thin sandy hair lay plastered dank with sweat.

A sick man! Pallid, gasping as though now under my attack his breath was choking him. I saw that he was a man of about fifty. Dying of some desperate illness? Certainly he looked it.

"Oh, Uncle Joe," Dolly murmured, "you're all right now? Just lie quiet."

"Your Uncle?" I echoed.

"No. My—my father's best friend. I've always called him Uncle Joe. He—he took care of me when my father and mother died—"

His eyes were closed. For a moment I thought that he was dead. Then his lids raised; he was gasping again and his bloodless lips were trying to smile at the girl. Captain Allaire for the moment was ignoring us. He was at the chart-room window; then he dashed to the turret, fired through one of the slits there, making sure that none of the bandits took advantage of this turmoil here by trying to rush us. But it seemed quiet now outside.

And then Dolly, with murmured, only half coherent words, was babbling out her pathetic little story. Trigger Joe—his name was Joe Johnson. When Dolly was a child he had taken care of her. She had not known then that he was a criminal. Then she had grown up; gone on the stage and television; became self-supporting. Johnson's criminal activities were over. He was stricken with a heart ailment—dilation of the heart. Incurable; he would die in a few years.

And ever since then the girl, knowing finally about his past, had supported him in an Earth-hideout. He was penniless and she had worked for him, trying to care for him.

I stared blankly. How I had misjudged this mystery on the ill-fated little *Stardust!* Trigger Joe certainly was not our adversary here!

When he came abroad he had known nothing of the plot to gain possession of the cylinder of Concentrate-27!

He was recovering a little now. His burning, fevered eyes with love for the girl in them, turned to me. "She—was always very good to me," he murmured. "Worked so hard for me—terrible strain on her—frightened always that the New York Shadow Squad men would spot me."

And then he was telling me things that even the girl did not know. He had decided to smuggle himself to Mars. A stow-away here on the *Stardust,* and Dolly was making the trip to be with him.

"She thinks I was afraid I'd be spotted in New York. Well, I was." He tried to grin at me with irony. "But it was more than that. You see, there's no reward for me on Earth. But on Mars—four decimars— that would be forty thousand Earth-dollars. A lot of money—if I'm caught alive in Martian territory."

I KNEW that custom. Foreign criminals on Earth—always a big reward if you can take them alive. And Earth-criminals on Mars, the same. And so Johnson, with his expanded, bursting heart, had been trying to stay alive until he could reach Martian territory. And then he would make Dolly turn him over to the authorities and have her claim the reward.

"Oh," she gasped. "I—I had no idea of that."

"Dying anyway, what difference?" he murmured with his faint smile. "She—she deserves it, Allen—that money—it will make her—secure for life, you see?"

Allaire momentarily was with us. He got the gist of what we were saying. "But the cylinder—the Concentrate-27," he demanded.

"Cylinder?" Johnson echoed. He was sitting up now, with a little strength coming back to him. "A small cylinder? Why, there it is—"

He gestured. Over in the chart-room corner, where he had been crouching when I attacked him, the small lead cylinder lay propped against the wall! I jumped and inspected it. The Concentrate-27 was here, unharmed!

And now, with what Johnson was telling us, we could piece together the plot of the murderous double-crossing Purser. Johnson had come upon Franklin opening the safe, taking out the cylinder, and then fusing the safe-lock, cracking it with a little heat-torch. And

Franklin had with him a duplicate cylinder—a fake package of the Concentrate-27. He took it to a corner of the corridor; carefully hid the fake package behind a fire extinguisher. And he was making off with the real cylinder when Johnson jumped him.

Johnson was grinning at me. "Nice idea, trying to do something decent, just for once as you're dying—"

I saw now that in the fight, as he had forced his way up here with the cylinder, he had been drilled through the shoulder.

"Franklin was trying to double-cross somebody?" Allaire muttered.

"Of course," I exclaimed. "His principal, who was to make the get-away. He took the fake package. Franklin figured he wouldn't discover it until he was too far away to return. And Franklin would have the bribe which had been given him, plus the real treasure!"

But the Purser's plan had been thwarted by Johnson. And Franklin had been searching to find Trigger Joe and get back the cylinder. With his chief returning because the volplane failed to operate, the best Franklin could do was alibi himself that Trigger Joe had substituted the fake package. Doubtless he had alibied already!

"Damned dirty villain," Captain Allaire burst out. "He's down there on the forepeak now. I've tried a dozen times to drill him."

As though to answer the words, we heard the splatter of a bolt as it struck one of the turret window-blinds. Down on the dim, blood-red forepeak we could vaguely see the prone figure of the murderous Purser, lying behind the cargo-loader. I flung a bolt down at him but it only brought his jibing laugh.

"Save your current," Allaire warned me. "Haven't much left in these Banning guns here. We'll have to build up re-charges—takes time, and if they find it out—"

Doubtless they knew that we could easily exhaust our gun-strength. Three of us here—though Johnson certainly didn't seem able to fight. And we had the girl. We tried to figure how many of the bandits were against us. The two big Martian deckhands. The Purser. And the man who had tried to make a getaway. I had seen a big black robed, hooded figure dart along the dim superstructure roof after the slaughter of the passengers started. The man in the burned cloak.

FOUR of them against us probably. And they had control of the ship.

From the lower control room all the mechanisms could be operated despite our controls here. And the main radio-helio sender was wrecked. A bolt had struck into it.

"I'm building up current in our batteries here for the emergency sender," Allaire told me. "If we can only hold out, Allen. In an hour I'll have power. We'll send a helio-distress. By God, if that goes out there'll be a patrolship after us."

Did the bandits know that we could do that? If they did, undoubtedly they would try to rush us.

A buzz sounded in the turret—the direct-voice tube from the hull control room. Allaire answered it.

"Hello—what you want?"

"That you, Captain?" The voice of the bandit down there in the hull control room was blurred and muffled by the tube. There was no familiar sound to it. "Don't you think you better surrender, Captain? We promise you won't be killed—" There was a chuckle. "We're going to the Dark Country of Mars. You can't stop us, you know—and we want that cylinder from you now."

"You go to hell," Allaire roared. "Kill us? We'll kill every damn one of you before this is through. You murderous, double-crossing—"

"Empty threats, Captain. You're helpless. Even worse, because you see—"

I suddenly felt my throat constricting; my nostrils stinging. The choleric, red-faced Allaire at the voice-tube suddenly coughed and staggered, clutching at the turret wall for support.

"Ventilators!" he gasped. "Allen, quick! Shut them off!"

Johnson and Dolly were here; Johnson on his feet looking like a walking dead man. Both of them were gasping, coughing.

From our ventilators chlorine fumes were pouring up from below! I jumped and snapped them closed. Did the same in the chart-room. Through the chart-room window-slit, sternward over the dim starlit superstructure roof I saw the crouching figure of one of the big Martian deckhands, watching his chance to rush us. I took a shot at him and he jumped up and scurried away.

"We'll have to open the windows a bit," Allaire gasped.

We raised them all about a foot. The ship's air from the forepeak and the superstructure roof drifted in to us. They couldn't very well poison that air without poisoning themselves.

"Not so pleasant, was it?" the ironic voice from the tube was saying. "And food and water—you'll begin to miss them pretty soon, won't you?"

"Go to the devil," I shouted into the tube and closed it off.

Johnson swayed against me. "You better sit down," I admonished.

"No—don't want to. If they—rush us—you give me a gun." His whimsical grin still was on his lips. "I'm still very handy with a gun—I've had lots of practice—they called me Trigger Joe, you know."

I shoved one into his hand. He staggered, but he gripped it, with practiced fingers caressing it. "That feels natural, Allen. Sure does. I certainly hope they—rush us."

They did. They knew, of course, that we were building power to send a distress call. And if that went out over the star-ways and a patrolship picked it up, they'd have a pretty tough time getting away with this bandit vessel. I should have been warned perhaps, at a glimpse of a black blob climbing up under the glassite dome almost over the turret. But I held my shot; our charges were low—we did not dare waste gun-current now.

And suddenly from the turret there came Allaire's shout. "By God, they're coming—"

It was all from the forepeak. The figure of the murderous Purser appeared on the turret-balcony ladder. Allaire's bolt missed him, and he dropped back. A big brown Martian already was on the balcony which encircled the front of the turret! And then the Purser's bolt sizzled through one of our window slits! It struck Captain Allaire full in the chest, drilled through him with the nauseous smell of charred flesh as he tumbled backward.

"Why—why here they are!" Johnson muttered. He went staggering past me, shoved the turret door open and staggered out to the balcony. The Martian out there was so suddenly startled that he ripped out an oath and jumped for the forepeak. It was a ten foot drop. Johnson's bolt caught him on the wing. Like a bird in midair the hurtling Martian crumpled. He was dead, charred leprous with part of his face gone, when he struck the deck. Trigger Joe certainly could shoot!

The Purser had leaped from behind the little cargo-loader. Cowardly damned villain, but he thought this was his chance. My gun leaped level. But Johnson's shot caught him in the heart before I could fire.

Hardly more than twenty tumultuous seconds. Behind me in the turret, Dolly was screaming with an agony of terror. From the balcony Johnson came lurching back. Gasping for breath, his poor bloated heart laboring. A dead man, fighting on his feet. But he was grinning.

"Sure feels natural," he muttered. "Dolly, don't be a fool—screaming like this—"

AND then we both saw why she was screaming. The trap-door exit-port in the turret ceiling had slid aside. A dark cloaked figure up there came leaping down; landed on my back, crushing me under it. The panting, gasping Johnson was barely able to stand on his feet. I heard him curse as he tried to shove Dolly aside.

The man in the burned cloak. He was sprawled on me now. A black hood muffled his face.

"Got you now, Allen—" he muttered.

But he didn't have me. *My* gun had clattered away with the impact of his body knocking me down. He had a gun that he was trying to jab against my head, but my flailing fist hurtled it from his grip. And then I lunged from under him.

I was aware in that chaotic instant that the remaining Martian deckhand had come through the chart-room. Johnson seemed to have fallen; out on his feet. But as he went down, his bolt stabbed up. The oncoming Martian caught it between the eyes, tumbled dead in the center of the turret. And then Johnson was trying to fire at my antagonist. His gun clicked; it was de-charged; useless. With a curse he flung it away. It slid along the floor and as I lay entangled, wrestling with the black-cloaked murderer, the sliding gun hit my hand. Johnson had intended it; and I seized the gun, cracked it down on the black hood. The big sprawling, lunging body went suddenly limp in my arms. I tore away the black hood.

Mantell the Magician! J. Tarkington Mantell, suave and genial passenger on the little *Stardust!* Gracious Interplanetary traveler, former theatrical man, skilled with scientific illusions to fool an audience! Scientific magic! With what irony he had told us, as we sat on the *Stardust's* forepeak, that scientific magic could fool anyone! Could make things seem what they are not! I remembered that little crackling hissing, down between my chair and Mantell's. And then the purple ball of ionized air had appeared! Conjured by some electric apparatus Mantell was using!

He lay here now with blood streaming from his head where I had cracked him. And there was a knife-wound in his chest—some member of our loyal crew who had put up a fight before getting killed. Mantell was not dead, but dying, quite obviously. His glazing eyes focused on me. Bloody foam welled at his lips, but he was trying to smile.

"I told you—Allen—science-magic can do—wonderful things if you have the skill. Mantell the magician—a very skillful fellow in his line. Wasn't hard to—terrorize the crew—so we'd put in at the asteroid."

A gush of blood from his lips choked him, but he struggled on. "And that space-storm. That wasn't exterior disturbance. It was my—electric-magic. Deranged, free-running static-electricity—the sort of thing I used to use a lot in my—stage work. It certainly threw the ship into chaos, didn't it? Nice stake I was after, Allen—could have sold that concentrate for nearly a thousand decimars. Ten million Earth-dollars—that's what the Dark Country Martians would have paid—"

His mouth filled with blood. Then he was twitching, with a final gurgling rattle in his throat. He was still trying ironically to smile, thinking of the trickery of his science-magic, as the light went out of his eyes and he was gone.

Here on the turret floor I felt Johnson plucking at me. "Guess that was the end of them, eh, Allen?"

"Yes. Undoubtedly."

Charnel ship of death. It was silent now, strewn with carnage. Just three of us here. And Johnson was dying; no question of that. He lay here on the floor; a bluish tinge was coming to his chalk-white pallor.

"You must—send out that call for help," he murmured. "Isn't the battery strength enough yet?"

I checked it. "Almost," I said.

Dolly had brought a cushion for his head. "You're all right now, dear. Just lie quiet—you've had these attacks before."

"Not quite like this, Dolly."

WE GOT him up onto the Captain's bunk in the chart-room presently. Then I sent the call, repeating it at intervals. And then at last I contacted an Earth patrolship. It answered. It would come and convoy us to Mars.

"Why, that's good," Johnson agreed. He was visibly weaker now. Fighting to keep alive. And suddenly his groping hand pulled me down to him. "Got to stay alive," he murmured. "We're not in the Martian Mandate Zone yet, are we, Allen?"

"No, not quite."

"Got to stay alive till we get there. Then you can—report that you've captured 2Y-X-4-4. Report that you've caught him—alive in Martian spaceways. They'll take your word for that—you're an official—" His glazing eyes were pleading with me. "Then Dolly will get the reward, you see? Got to stay alive for that."

The capture of 2Y-X-4-4! Earth and Mars, and Venus too, would ring with the news, within an hour. Trigger Joe captured alive.

"That's just fine, Allen. Thanks."

"You like her a lot, don't you, Allen?" he murmured.

I nodded.

His groping hand fumbled at his face. His queer hooked nose—his high cheekbones. Wax-disguise! His nails drew blood in the skin—but in a moment the disguise was gone. His face had changed. Gaunt pallid face. But now it was a replica of my own, grown older!

My father! I gasped, numbed as I stared and then bent down over him. And his faint voice was telling me: he had not been guilty of that crime when he disappeared. He had been kidnapped with the treasure he had been guarding; taken to a distant world. Years later, he had escaped. Couldn't find me or mother. And then, with the cloud of guilt on him, he had become Trigger Joe…

"Jon, lad," he was murmuring, "it's good to be with you—now at the end—you—take care of Dolly always—fine girl, Dolly—always so good to me. I'm glad you both are—going to have the reward—"

Alone in the turret starlight I sat with Dolly, staring out through the bow-dome where Mars hung, dull-red disc among the stars.

THE THOUGHT MACHINE

Butch Conners, with Red and Willie at his elbow, crouched in the alley peering through the window into the dim eerie laboratory. The two men in there were standing before a weird-looking apparatus that glistened blue-green in the light.

"Where's the safe?" Willie murmured.

The safe of the wealthy Dr. Jenks didn't seem to be here; or if it was Conners couldn't see it. The window was up a little at the bottom; the voices of the two men inside were audible.

"I call it a Thought-machine," Dr. Jenks was saying. "I've been working on it many years, and it's perfected now—just tonight. There's nothing new, as you know, John, in the scientific theory that thought is actually a tangible vibration. Infinitely tiny, infinitely rapid vibration of the ether, perhaps. That idea was scientifically postulated, back around 1900."

"To account for thought-transference," the other man said. "Someone whose brain happens to be a receiving station for your own particular thought-vibrations—"

"Exactly," Dr. Jenks said warmly. "But I haven't been working on that angle of it. I am convinced, John, that somewhere—call it in a Fourth Dimension if you like—there exists what might be termed a Realm of Unthought Things. A vast storehouse of energy—mental energy. A realm co-existing with ours—unperceived by us because it has a different basic vibration-rate. The great Creator's storehouse. We fatuous humans believe that when we think a thing out—solve some knotty problem—devise something new—discover something—invent a new process or machine—we believe, John, that we have created something. What nonsense! Everything has been created by Omnipotence. All we are doing, scientifically, is sending our questing vibrations of thought out into what, to us, is the Unknown. They reach that realm—that storehouse—derive a new energy there. And come back to us, amplified, and our brain receives them, translates them into what we call Knowledge. We have brought something out of the Realm of Unthought Things—"

"The place where everything is waiting to be thought of," the other man murmured with awe. "If only you could prove—"

"I have, John. A year ago, I saw it. My little apparatus—it was so delicate that its own energy burned it up in a moment. But I caught the radiations of that storehouse. They bathe our realm constantly. They stimulate our brains—our quest for knowledge, we call it. But, scientifically, it's only the physical impact of vibrations against our brain—stimulating our own thought-waves. I made those incoming vibrations visible, for just an instant, John—as one makes visible the bombardment of a cathode-ray tube, to get a television image. I saw the realm of Unthought Things! And now this machine I've just finished will take me there!"

In the alley outside the laboratory window, Willie murmured impatiently, "Butch, listen, I don't see no safe in there. Hadn't we better—"

* * * *

Conners silenced him with a muttered oath. By what these men were saying, that Thought-machine might be pretty valuable—more valuable than what was supposed to be in Dr. Jenks' safe. And then a weird idea came to the squat, beetle-browed Butch Conners. It was so weird it gave him the creeps. But he clung to it because it might be possible. My Gawd what a stake to play for! A million dollars? Why, that would be nothing compared to what they could rake in if they pulled off a stunt like this! . . .

Within the laboratory, with the lurid blue-green sheen of light glistening on the weird little apparatus, the two men went on talking. Dr. Jenks was explaining to his friend now how the Thought-machine worked. So simple. Conners, with the lanky young Red and the weazel-faced little Willie beside him, listened intently, eagerly, to what the men inside were saying. So simple to work; Conners was memorizing it now. My Gawd what a haul they'd make! . . .

Luck is a wonderful thing. Conners had always had it; and it stayed with him now. Within half an hour—it was midnight now—Dr. Jenks and his friend left the laboratory; within another hour they planned to use the little Thought-machine, starting upon their weird trip.

"Now's our chance," Conners whispered. "Red, stand down there at the end of the alley. Get inside, Willie—hand that damned thing out to me."

In every job it was the agile Willie who went up the waterpipe or through the window. He handed out the Thought-machine silently and skillfully. Red made sure that nobody saw them as they hoisted it over the alley wall, and ran to their parked car at the edge of the empty lot.

"Well, we got it," Red said dubiously. "What in the hell will we do with it? You think Sam'll pay anything for it? Listen, there ain't a fence in the city who'll touch that fool thing with a ten foot pole. If there ever was a piece of hot goods—"

They were safely in Conner's lodging house room.

"We're not gonna sell it," Conners declared. "Not for a million. Now listen, you mugs—"

Patiently, he explained. The Realm of Unthought Things. Where it was, Conners had no very clear idea. But it was a hidden place, somewhere near here because Dr. Jenks had said this machine would take you to it in what would seem maybe only half an hour. A place where unthought things were hidden. Things like the world's first locomotive, for instance. That had been there and it was here now.

"Listen," Conners was saying earnestly, "maybe you don't get the science of this, but it's simple enough. In this Realm of Unthought Things all the great inventions of the future are lyin' stored. Any one of 'em's worth a million bucks."

"Inventions—such as what?" Willie demanded.

Conners gave him a withering look. "Don't be an idiot. They haven't been thought of yet. How can I describe 'em to you?"

"I get you," the lanky Red put in. "We go there an' get 'em an' bring 'em back—and sell 'em."

It was an amazing idea, but how simple, once you thought of it. "You see," Conners explained, "like he said, this here Thought-machine bathes you in its rays—vibrations or somethin'. Then you get changed, and you go there an' the machine goes with you."

* * * *

All the intricacies of science, no doubt, might be reduced like that to naked essentials. Dr. Jenks had talked, with considerable detail, concerning the transmutation of the human body atoms—and the atoms of the Thought-machine itself—into a different state of matter. The scientific state, of which thoughts are composed. We call the state, mental—because it is different from what we know as physical. But it has an existence; as tangible as our physical world, to do anything of its own vibration-rate.

Dr. Jenks expounded with a wealth of incontrovertible detail— but all Butch Conners got was the naked, practical fact that here was some place to which you could go, get something valuable and bring it back. (Most of us accept life's scientific wonders with exactly that stark realism. We talk over the telephone; listen to the radio; view the television. And we press a button when we want electric light. Butch Conners was equally practical; it is results that count.)

"I got it all memorized," Conners was saying. "Stand away— give me room an' I'll hook it up. We might's well get goin'."

In their squalid lodging house room, the weird little Thought-machine stood dark and inert, glum and stolid. It was a box-like affair, some two feet cube, mounted on a small wheeled chassis. All its six square faces were plastered with dials, levers and little intricate wire grids. It carried its own batteries, Conners explained. Three wire belts were fastened to it. Conners unhooked them. He put one around his waist; and each of his companions did the same. Then they each selected two wires, and hooked them to their belt. The wires came out of the Thought-machine with a springlike tension.

"We wheel the damned little thing between us," Conners was explaining. "The wires give us about six feet to move around in."

A little knowledge is such a dangerous thing! The Thought-machine stood glum and inert; but presently Conners was fumbling at its starting lever.

"Give it a good shove," Willie urged.

There was a buzz down in the vitals of the weird dark cube, and abruptly it sprang into life—whirring, clicking with a blue-green, violet, red and orange radiance coming to it. The light bathed Conners' room with an eerie glare; bathed the three men who stood with their feet braced. And it permeated the Thought-machine itself so that now, for just a second Conners seemed to see it as a thing alive, monstrously expanding, turning ghost-like . . .

Then Conners was aware of a shock that sent him to the floor in darkness, with Willie and Red on top of him. And then everything went black. Had he fainted?

"Butch, where are you?" It was Willie's frightened voice. He found Willie gripping him in the darkness. Red was here, floating, futilely kicking. Where was the Thought-machine? Conners couldn't see it, but he could seem to feel that he was attached to it and that it was floating here with them.

"My Gawd," Red was faintly murmuring. "I didn't know you felt like this when you were dead."

* * * *

For just a moment it occurred to Butch Conners that he was sorry to have committed suicide like this. They were in a vast abyss of blackness. But there was movement here—gigantic movement of the blackness rushing forward at them, passing to the sides and closing in behind. And then he realized that they were speeding forward. Rushing with the speed of thought. That was it! Dr. Jenks had said it would be something like that. This was the journey; they were on their way!

"What the hell are you scared of?" Conners murmured contemptuously to his two companions. "Everything's okay. Sit tight an' watch—we ought to be gettin' there pretty soon."

One may get used to anything. They seemed presently to be aware that they were standing together, wheeling the little machine beside them. They could see it vaguely; it looked inert and dark now; but Conners thought that he could vaguely hear it humming. He touched it and found that it was solid. Willie was solid and so was Red. But the abyss was a rushing shadow.

"Wonder what this Realm of Unthought Things will look like?" Conners muttered. "I should think it oughter be pretty big?"

Was there something in Conners' mind then—his thoughts of what he would see—making a reality here in this mental darkness? He murmured his ideas excitedly to Willie and Red and presently they all saw the tiny grey, luminous patch, infinitely far ahead of them in the giant distance. An expanding patch as it rushed forward at them, so that all in a moment it was widening out to the sides, above and below, and closing in behind them.

At first there was just a vast greyness, rushing past at railroad speed. And then the grey was taking form; blurred outlines, like mountains of fog in a foggy sky. They were everywhere now, rushing, hurtling in a vast tumbling cataclysm. Then Conners could see valleys between them; and then he realized that the Thought-machine was hurling them into just one valley. Its canyon-like walls were moving more slowly now. Other valleys were visible; and as the speed of everything gradually slackened, there were rifts; pits, and grey cave-mouths.

Avenues into which each of us may probe with his thoughts . . . But Butch Conners knew nothing of that. He was aware only that Red and Willie seemed tugging at him now, as though trying to go a little in some other direction so that he turned upon them angrily:

"Hey, listen, you two—stay with me, dammit."

"I don't see no inventions," Willie muttered. He had his feet planted wide, for a brake against the backward-rushing greyness beneath them. He was staring into the greyness of a shadowy grotto that drifted slowly past. "Say, that's funny," he muttered. "That looks like the back room of Mike's Bar an' Grill. Damn if it doesn't."

Now that should have warned Butch Conners, but it didn't. Red was silently staring into a little window-like cave-mouth. A foolish grin came to his handsome, slack-jawed face; and he sucked in his breath as though with pleasure at something he thought he saw.

But Conners was thinking only of fabulously valuable inventions. The idea would be to pick some small ones. Good goods come in small packages. That crack was true enough. You couldn't tell the value by the size. Pick small ones and you could carry a lot.

"Well, we're here," Conners said suddenly. There was no doubt of it. The movement had ceased. Everything was solid here now—solid grey ground under them; grey rocks, grey walls of this vast grotto in which now Conners could see that they were standing.

* * * *

The Realm of Unthought Things! What an amazing place! Everywhere he looked, vast dim corridors stretched off into the grey distance. And every corridor had others branching from it—a million corridors and yet other millions . . . And every corridor had rooms where shadowy things were piled. Vast rooms with millions upon millions of things in each of them. No, that was wrong. Some of the rooms were empty, where things had been taken out. Everything in the world was here once, and people had gotten some of it out . . .

But certainly there was enough left. Maybe more than half. And no cops here to guard it. What a cinch! You just stepped up and took what you liked.

Into Conners' vague but eager contemplation of a loot, unguarded here, that could run into billions of dollars, came Willie's voice:

"Don't seem to be nothin' much here, does there?"

Queer how anybody could say that, when everything that ever would be in the world, was right here!

"You're nuts," Conners muttered. "Everything's here. Let's take a look in this room—see what we want an' grab it."

He wheeled the little Thought-machine forward and dragged Willie and Red along with him. Shadowy things were piled in the gigantic room. Conners could see vast shelves on which grey things were stacked. Millions of things, all standing in neat rows—endless rows one over the other, extending in every direction back into an endless shadowy distance. He went up to one shelf. He stared at just one thing on the shelf. Here was something that might be valuable.

Queer. The thing lay right here before him. When he glanced at it casually it seemed to be a little mechanism of some valuable invention. But now, as he gazed at it to see its details, at once it seemed to be formless, elusive, almost as though nothing was there at all.

Butch Conners stood tense, puzzled, baffled. Damn the thing. And then he reached out to touch it. That was queer too. The thing was here, but as though it was only a vague grey mist—or something not even that solid—his hand went through it, feeling nothing. Wasn't the Thought-machine working? What the devil was the matter?

"Hey lookit! My Gawd, there's Whitey O'Neill!" Conners felt Willie gripping him; and Willie's voice was an excited squeal of fear. "He sees us, Butch! My Gawd, he's pulled his gat on us!"

Red gasped out an oath; and he too was gripping Conners. All three of them tensely stared; and they all saw it. The shadowy recess here was quite obviously the little back room of Mike's Bar and Grill, heavy as always with dangling layers of grey-blue tobacco smoke. The window was open at the bottom. Whitey O'Neill, his tight-lipped mouth grim, his eyes blazing with menace, was there staring at them. And his hand at his hip held his automatic leveled!

"Duck!" Willie hissed in terror. "He's gonna let us have it now, like he always said he would!"

To anyone who conceivably is in the Fourth Dimension, everything else there must of necessity be real. To a shadow, another shadow must of necessity be a thing of substance, perhaps the most substantial thing existing in all the universe. And who shall say it is not also so in our own three-dimensional world—the very existence of which is only conjured by the blended impressions of our five mortal senses? Who can know, apart from our conjuring thoughts, that anything exists at all? To Butch Conners, Willie and Red in that startling moment, there could be no question of the reality of that window of Mike's Bar and Grill; no question of the reality of the murderous Whitey O'Neill, with his three henchmen of the Downtown Mob behind him.

* * * *

The Realm of Unthought Things! Whatever it had been a moment ago, it was a bedlam of familiar things now . . . The shabby little street was dim; there was no traffic and only one lone pedestrian furtively lurking at the distant corner of the avenue. One of the Downtown Mob probably.

"Well, you had it coming to you—say your prayers." Whitey's smooth ironic voice, dripping like ice-water with murderous menace, sounded in the stillness. His voice mingled with the tinny sound of a piano rattling out swing music which came from another window in the front room of Mike's. Red had been staring in there a moment ago, absorbed with a girl who was swaying to the music with hands on her hips and a cigarette dangling from her rouged lips. Conners could see her now out of the tail of his eye.

"Don't move, you'll get it all the quicker," Whitey's voice was ironically saying. "Just say your prayers—"

And Conners didn't have his gun with him; nor did Red; nor Willie! Caught like rats in a trap! But Whitey didn't fire. The sound of a police siren split the night air. An oncoming radio car! And then another! People were at every window now. Staring down. Shouting.

The lone man at the Avenue corner was running away, scurrying like a rat. From behind Whitey in the window of Mike's Bar and Grill, one of his damfool mob fired a shot. It went wild; splintered the window glass at the top. Whitey muttered a curse and vanished from the window.

The whole place in there was a turmoil; oaths of men; the screams of women, drinking at the bar and at the tables. Then they were pouring out into the street in a panic . . . The first of the radio cars came howling around the avenue corner, almost on two wheels. Shots began coming from it; a fusillade of gunfire with yellow-red spurts of flame. The leaden slugs splattered the street.

In the midst of the chaos, Conners gripped his two companions convulsively and then shoved at them. "Come on," he muttered. "Get away from here—"

Red was staring up to where a girl with not much on had come running out onto a fire escape, peering down at the turmoil. Then from inside Mike's shots were coming; Conners heard the whistle of one going past his ears. He was trying to run, but something stopped him. Something was tugging at his belt. The Thought-machine! He remembered that they were all connected to it by wires. No time to disconnect them.

"Wheel the damned little thing!" he muttered to Willie. "Have to roll it between us."

Red was still staring up at the girl on the fire escape. He had been muttering about her. Conners gave him a shove. With Willie he tried frantically to heave the little Thought-machine along. They were running away from the avenue around the corner of which the police car had arrived. It had pulled up in front of Mike's. Coppers were pouring out; running into Mike's. A big grey ambulance was coming now; it screamed as it pulled to a halt. White-coated internes leaped out from it.

* * * *

Then from ahead of Conners a fire engine came with its siren screaming and its bell clanging.

"Can't—go that way!" Willie panted. "Lookit—"

Ahead of them three radio cars had stopped. The whole little street there near the corner was jammed with policemen. Conners tried to duck into an areaway. He forgot Willie and Red; forgot the Thought-machine. The areaway had a flight of rickety steps down to a basement entrance under a butcher shop. Conners miscalculated the steps and catapulted down head first. There was a flash—a weird puff of soundless light all around him. He was aware that the little Thought-machine and its wheeled chassis had come tumbling down the steps after him—and that Red and Willie had broken their wires and kept on running up the street—running for a split second until the flash enveloped them.

There might have been a split second also when Conners knew that the Thought-machine had crashed into the areaway. And then his thoughts—his human consciousness, abnormal to this realm, out of tune here, dependent upon the vibrations of the apparatus for their very existence—went black, and there was nothing left of him or his universe as he was hurled away.

Science, or fantasy? Who shall say where one ends and the other begins? Are we not all of us, awake and asleep, questing into the Realm of Unthought Things? What Butch Conners, Willie and Red found there—conjured there if you like—was undoubtedly based upon their quality of thought-vibrations. From the vast storehouse of everything, their inherent thought-energy vibrations could only pick up the vibrations of certain things to which by nature they were at-tuned, transmuting them into reality—a definite reality, for Conners, Red and Willie.

And if *you* went there—what would you find? Everything is there. What would that little spark of nameless Something which is you, have the power to select? To create into *your* reality? Every instant we live, we are doing just that. Conjuring with the power of our thought—perceiving with our senses—what we think is the reality of this world outside us. How different it must be, to each of us! And, Heaven or Hell, we can make it what we will.

THE CURIOUS CASE OF NORTON HOORNE

CHAPTER 1

I do not feel that now, after these many years, it is any breach of professional etiquette for me to relate the case of Norton Hoorne. It was so remarkable, so extraordinary an incident, that it seems wrong to let it lie forever buried in the professional secrecy to which my good friend, the late Dr. Johns, consigned it. And so now, after nearly twenty years, I have decided to give my remembrance of the events just as they occurred.

I attempt no explanation. I am not psychic. Indeed, I know very little of the subject, for it is not one that appeals to me. I have never seen a ghost, nor have I ever talked with any one who had. You who read this may explain it as you will. I shall merely set down for you the plain facts; and if, by so doing, I shall have added anything of value to the existing data on Psychical Research, I shall be amply repaid.

At the time the incidents occurred, I remember, I had just taken my medical degree. My mother had wanted me to become a musician. I was, and in fact always have been, tremendously interested in music. But the career of professional pianist, for it was that branch of the art to which I leaned, seemed to hold little promise for a youth whose talent obviously fell far short of genius, so I decided upon the medical profession instead.

At the time I took my degree I had two friends who meant a great deal to my life. They were Dr. Johns and Norton Hoorne, the latter one of the most famous concert pianists in the country. The friendship of these two men, and the inspiration I derived from them both, was the biggest thing in my life at this period—excepting possibly my interest in my work.

It was in the spring of 1900, I remember, that Dr. Johns and I attended one of Hoorne's concerts in New York. I know we were both proud, as we sat in that huge, enthusiastic audience, to feel we were the closest friends of such a man.

Norton Hoorne was at this time at the very pinnacle of his fame. He was about thirty-five years of age—a most picturesque figure, tall and straight, with very black wavy hair slightly touched with gray at the temples. His features were strong—almost rugged. Yet his mouth was sensitive as a girl's, and his face, for all its sturdy strength, was the face of a poet. He had never married, but lived alone in his luxurious studio on Riverside Drive with an old housekeeper who was devoted to him.

Hoorne was unquestionably a great artist. But we knew him also as a great man—a man big mentally, physically and spiritually; had he been otherwise the events I am about to relate might have been less inexplicable.

I think it was hardly two or three days after the concert that Dr. Johns called me up one morning shortly after breakfast.

"Something has happened," he explained hurriedly. "Norton's housekeeper has just phoned me. Will you come right up to his studio?"

Then he hung up without waiting for me to reply.

When I arrived I was ushered in at once by the frightened housekeeper. She took me immediately to the studio and I found Dr. Johns already there. He led me across the room without a word and pointed to the grand piano that stood in a corner by the window. On the bench before it sat Norton Hoorne, his body sprawled forward over the keyboard of the instrument.

How curious it is, that in moments of great mental stress little details impress themselves upon one's mind that in other times would pass unnoticed! I can remember the scene in Hoorne's studio that morning as though it had happened yesterday. It was a luxurious room, in perfect order now as always. Large French windows opened onto the Drive, and by the piano stood a many-pillowed divan where frequently I had lain and listened to Hoorne's playing.

Dr. John's had arrived but a short while before, and now in a few words he told me what had happened as far as he knew it. Hoorne was not dead as I had supposed by my first hurried glance, but was in a most extraordinary state of catalepsy. There was absolutely no sign of life except in so far as there was also no positive sign of death. Both pulse and respiration apparently had ceased.

We lifted our friend from his position at the piano and laid him prone upon the divan. Dr. Johns had not wanted to move him, he said, until I arrived. I had a dozen horrified questions to ask, but he would have none of them. I could see by his manner that he knew, or suspected, the cause of Hoorne's condition. And because he wished it so, I questioned no more, but helped him with his further examination.

When we had finished, at his request, I summoned the housekeeper. The poor woman came at once; she was frightened almost out of her wits and was crying softly.

"Did Mr. Hoorne have his dinner here last evening?" Dr. Johns began at once.

"Yes, sir, he did."

"Alone?"

"Yes, sir."

"You told me you did not notice he was ill?"

"No, sir, he ate very well."

"What did he do after dinner?"

"Came right up here, sir. I think he spent the first part of the evening reading."

I looked over the few books scattered on top of the library table. Lying under the electrolier I found an opened volume of Freud's Psychoanalysis, several sheets of music, and two or three operatic scores. I picked up the volume of Freud and showed it to Dr. Johns.

"Very probably," he said, and continued his questions.

"You retired about half past eight?"

"Yes, sir."

"And very soon afterward you heard Mr. Hoorne begin playing?"

"Very soon after; yes, sir."

"How long did he play?"

"I don't know, sir; I fell asleep listening to him."

Dr. Johns looked at her curiously. "Do you know anything about music?" he asked.

The housekeeper smiled a little through her tears. "I ought to, sir, I've been with Mr. Hoorne a long time."

"I know you have—yes. What sort of music was it he was playing?"

The old lady thought a moment. "I don't rightly think I can say, sir," she replied. "I don't remember he played anything I had ever heard before."

"If he had played any ordinary piece—anything in his repertoire, or those he sometimes plays for diversion—would you have recognized it?"

"Yes, sir; I think so, sir—though I might not know its name."

"But you are familiar with most of the standard pieces, aren't you?" pursued the doctor.

"I know a great many—I do love music," she added earnestly, and her eyes filled with tears again as she looked at the motionless figure on the divan.

"What about the music, Fred?" I asked impatiently.

Dr. Johns raised his hand deprecatingly. "I was just recalling a conversation I had with Norton last week. I'll tell you later." He turned back to the housekeeper who stood looking at her master with pleading eyes.

"Oh, sir," she burst out. "Isn't there something I can do? Is it right just to let him lie there? He isn't—oh, please tell me he isn't dead."

The doctor gently led her to a chair and sat her down.

"No," he said, "he isn't dead. And there's nothing we can do just now. Don't you worry too much—perhaps he's not in great danger. We were talking about the music," he went on. "What sort of music was it? Did you notice anything peculiar about it?"

"Yes, sir, I did, now that you mention it. It was very curious music, sir."

"How curious?"

"It was sort of weird, sir. I never heard anything like it before. One part of it gave me the creeps. And some of it sounded like discords, sir."

The doctor drew a long breath. "Thank you very much, Mrs. Beacon. I think that will do for now."

The housekeeper rose. "Yes, sir," she said. "And if there's anything I can do—oh, you will let me help, won't you, sir?" she pleaded.

"Yes, Mrs. Beacon, we will let you help," he answered kindly, and closed the door upon her pathetic figure.

"You know, Will," he said, turning back to me, "there's something mighty curious about this—I'm hanged if I understand it."

I was just about to reply when there happened the first of the extraordinary incidents that made this case so remarkable. I had just seated myself on the piano bench, with my back to the instrument. I remember I was leaning backward with my elbows resting on the music-ledge above the keyboard.

At Dr. Johns's remark I must have shifted my position slightly, for one of my elbows slipped off the rack and hit the keys with a thump, sending a crashing, jangling discord reverberating through the room. At the same instant there came a sharp rap from the floor near at hand. With the roots of my hair tingling, I turned toward the divan. Hoorne's right hand had slipped from his side to the floor, a large seal ring he wore striking sharply its polished surface. And as I looked at his face, I caught just the fleeting end of a convulsive jerk of the lips as they steadied again into immobility.

"Good God!" ejaculated Dr. Johns, as we started toward the divan. "Did you see that?"

We were both trembling violently as we examined the body. The convulsion had passed. Hoorne was in the same state of living death as before.

That was the first intimation I had of the connection of music with the case. What Dr. Johns knew and conjectured he was soon to tell me.

We were sitting beside the table, and Dr. Johns was idly fingering the volume of Freud.

"There's something mighty curious about this," he repeated slowly.

"You've some idea," I pursued, "or you wouldn't have talked to Mrs. Beacon that way."

"What I had in mind, Will," he answered, turning the leaves of the book in his hand—"you know how interested Norton was in psychic phenomena?"

"Of course."

"We were talking about it at the club a week or so ago. He confided something to me then—something he said he had never told anyone. It seems for some time he had been experimenting with a theory that through the power of a new style of music he had evolved, the soul could be transported temporarily out of its body and brought back at will. You know there are people who claim to be able to send their astral body with its soul wandering into other planes while their human body lies inert and helpless?"

"I know."

"Well, Norton said he had found that he could do just that by using certain kinds of music. I think I offended him a little, for I must have smiled rather skeptically. At any rate he wouldn't say much more except that he was afraid of the power he had acquired. I told him I thought that it might prove inconvenient when he was playing in public some time, and he replied quite seriously that was just what he feared. He seemed to be sorry that he had told me at all—just a little sheepish at my ridicule—and I couldn't get him to say any more. He asked me not to tell you about it."

Dr. Johns hesitated.

"Go on," I urged.

"That's all he said. Only—the look in his eyes made me know there was far more to it than that. Something so personal, so intimate, he could not even tell it to me."

Silence fell between us.

"And you think—" I prompted finally.

"What do *you* think? He was probably reading Freud last night. You heard what Mrs. Beacon said about the music. And now, when you happened to hit the piano—"

Dr. Johns stopped abruptly, his face very white, and for a long time we sat and stared at each other.

"What are we going to do about it?" I asked, breaking a silence that had become oppressive.

"We've got to assume, I think," Dr. Johns said, "that Norton's theory as he told it to me has turned to fact. He has forced or lured, or whatever you might term it, his astral body away to another plane. And for some reason it does not want to or cannot get back."

In spite of the seriousness of the situation, and the intense, earnest expression on my friend's face, I could not help smiling just a little at hearing such words from the lips of a man so coldly scientific as he.

"Do you believe that?" I asked when he paused.

"What else can I believe?" he answered. "At least it is a theory that fits the facts. Norton may have been experimenting with this thing for some time. God knows how far along he got with it—what he was able to do."

We tried to discuss the matter calmly; but to us it was so gruesome a subject, so darkly mysterious, so weird, that in spite of our efforts we found ourselves frequently at the point of becoming unnerved. There had been no change whatever in the body on the divan; it remained as before in a state that was the complete simulation of death.

I do not know what feelings caused us both to avoid suggesting the obvious thing to do. I think perhaps it was the almost supernatural aspect of the incident when I had unwittingly sounded a discord from the piano that made us hesitate to repeat it.

It was Dr. Johns who voiced first what was in both our thoughts.

"Whatever else may be in doubt," he began, "one thing is clear. Music has some definite connection with Norton's condition. It is to music we must look for a solution."

"How?" I asked.

"You know a great deal about music," he replied; "we shall have to experiment."

I jumped to my feet impulsively and struck a chord on the piano. I do not know what I expected, but my heart was beating furiously as the room vibrated with the music. I turned toward the divan; the body lay motionless as before.

Dr. Johns drew a chair beside the divan and sat down, staring steadily at Hoorne's face. "Try another," he said.

I played several chords in both major and minor keys; there was no effect whatever upon the body. With a sudden inspiration I turned around and rested my elbows on the music-ledge. Then I brought one of them sharply down upon the black keys. Simultaneously with the discord came a piercing shriek, followed by a low, mumbling groan, the most hideous, horrible sound I have ever heard issue from human lips.

When I got to the divan the body was lying on its side, the knees drawn closely up to the chest. I caught a glimpse of the contorted, agonized face. Then, with a convulsive jerk the legs straightened, the face relaxed. It was as though nothing had occurred, save that now the body was lying on its side, with one of its arms still hanging down, and the hand lying limply upon the floor.

Nothing else of importance happened that morning; the body remained motionless, and we were too unnerved to try any further experiments. We pulled down the shades and sat beside the divan, looking into the placid, ghastly white face of our friend, and talking together in low tones. Occasionally Dr. Johns would jump up and begin nervously to pace up and down the room, only to drop back in his chair again after a moment.

About noon the housekeeper timidly knocked on the door and brought us lunch. Dr. Johns agreed with me that until we considered it vitally necessary we should not call in any assistance, for publicity of this character would be extremely harmful to Hoorne's career. We decided therefore to carry the case through ourselves, and cautioned Mrs. Beacon to say nothing to the servants beyond the fact that their master was very ill, with two physicians in attendance.

We both felt better when we had eaten lunch. At Dr. Johns's request Mrs. Beacon and I brought down from one of the upper bedrooms a small cot. We undressed Hoorne and laid him on it, covering him to his neck with its white counterpane. Then dismissing the tearful, almost hysterical housekeeper with another admonition to say nothing concerning her master's condition, we prepared to carry out another experiment.

It was our plan—we had discussed it all very carefully at lunch—to begin with the faintest possible musical sounds, and find by trial those that would effect the body without causing the agony we had witnessed before.

Dr. Johns sat at the bedside and I at the piano began striking chord combinations as softly as I could. It was not until I had evolved what amounted practically to a discord that a sharp exclamation from Dr. Johns made me stop abruptly.

"Remember that," he commanded. "Play that again. Louder—a little louder." I doubled it with my left hand, striking it several times. An exclamation from my companion made me leave the piano and rush to his side.

"Look," he whispered; Hoorne's lips were moving, apparently trying to form words. Dr. Johns bent over him; then he straightened up and shook his head.

For over an hour we worked, trying every possible kind of music I could think of, but to no purpose; we got no further than this. Only one fact stood out plainly. The reactions the body gave were quite consistent; I could now almost anticipate the effect of my playing.

Then it occurred to me to look at the music we had found lying on the center table with the volume of Freud. The sheet music, that part of it that was in manuscript, I could tell even at first glance was like nothing I had ever seen before. It was not built upon the ordinary eight-note scale with its two whole tone intervals followed by a half tone, with which we are familiar. Perhaps it was based upon the old Chinese scale—I do not know.

One of the sheets was a composition of Debussy. There were some songs—one of them by Rimsky-Korsakow, I remember—and there was the pianoforte score of Moussorgsky's "Boris Godounov." Of this latter several pages were turned down at the corners. I opened at the places indicated and found many of the passages marked with a pencil, with penciled notations altering slightly the tempo and rhythm, and occasionally the harmony.

This music, which I found after a little practice I could play indifferently well, had far more effect upon the body than any I had hitherto been able to evolve. I played, with trembling fingers; Dr. Johns sat at the bedside, watching the effect of my music.

For some time I played, softly, haltingly. The body of Norton Hoorne, I could see it from where I sat playing, jerked convulsively. The face twitched and from the lips issued occasional heart-rending cries that were almost more than we could bear.

Then all at once there came a death-like silence. The body on the bed lay quiet. A sharp exclamation from Dr. Johns made me stop playing; in a moment I was by his side, leaning over the bed. Hoorne's lips were moving. We held our breaths, bending closer. From the lips came the sound of a low, mouthing muttering, and then the words distinctly audible:

"*It is all so useless.*"

I hardly know how to describe the tone in which these words were uttered. It had the quality I might best describe as *hollow*, a cold, measured, *detached* intonation, devoid absolutely of every quality of inflection—a voice forming words but embodying no human personality. I want to make this quite clear, because I think now that this detached quality, this *lack of personality* in the voice, was significant of much that subsequently happened.

Not only was the fact that Hoorne spoke startling in itself, but the weird, unearthly tones of his voice filled me with the utmost horror. I turned and fled back to the piano, in doubt whether to wait, or resume playing.

Then I heard Dr. Johns gently asking:

"What is all so useless?"

There was a long pause, and then in the same ghastly voice as before came the words:

"*Nothing matters now!*"

I sat down on the piano bench, and turning, caught a glimpse of the passive, livid face on the pillow, and Dr. Johns bending over it.

"What is all so useless?" he repeated. There was no answer, though we waited a long time, with our beating hearts audible it seemed in the heaviness of the silence.

Then Dr. Johns signed me to go on playing, and for perhaps ten minutes I went over and over the themes, elaborating them at times as fancy led me.

"Stop!" called the doctor sharply; I ceased abruptly, my hands poised above the keyboard.

"Play slowly, very softly," he commanded, and as I obeyed I heard his voice in the gentle tones one uses toward a child, asking, "Can you speak now, Norton?"

A long pause and then came the answer:

"*Yes.*"

"What can we do to help you?"

There was no answer.

"What can we do to help you, Norton?" repeated Dr. Johns. "Play louder," he added aside to me.

"*It is all so useless*," said the voice, louder and stronger than before. I let my playing die down a little.

"Why is it all so useless? Why is it, Norton?" asked Dr. Johns firmly and yet almost tenderly.

There was a longer pause than usual, and then came the words:

"*So useless. So useless, because she is not here—you must not make me live.*"

I do not know whether I played wrongly at this point or that it was merely from some other cause, but immediately after uttering these words the body was seized with a convulsion horrible to witness. I heard Dr. Johns's sharply indrawn breath and his muttered exclamation.

"Stop playing!" he commanded.

I did so, and hurried again to the bedside. The convulsion had ceased; the contorted face was relaxing.

"Why must we not make you live? Why, Norton?" Dr. Johns spoke almost in a whisper.

Standing directly over the bed I could see the muscles of the face as the lips parted and the words came forth.

"Because she has gone. I cannot reach her now."

And then a shudder seemed to pass over the entire body, and with more power than ever before the voice said:

"The desk. Look in the desk. Use it, for God's sake use it."

The body abruptly relaxed into immobility; we waited and waited, but there came nothing more.

That was the first we knew about the girl. On the desk stood a photograph—we had not noticed it before—in a small silver frame. It was the picture of a girl perhaps twenty-five years of age—a shy, beautiful face, with very large wistful eyes and a mass of golden hair. She was undeniably a girl of refinement and culture. The photograph showed her in what evidently was her own drawing-room. The fittings of the room were distinguishable, and the girl was seated with her back to a large grand piano, leaning an elbow upon the keyboard.

We took the photograph from its frame; there was nothing written upon it. Then we rummaged through the papers on the desk and came across a note written in a woman's small script. It gave an address in the East Sixties just off Fifth Avenue—one of the most fashionable sections of the city. It read simply:

> They wish it to be otherwise so—good-by.
>
> Elaine.

The note bore a date some three months previous to the time at which we read it.

We located the name of the family living in the palatial private residence at this address. It was the name of one of this country's most prominent financiers—you would remember it now if I were to mention it here. And I remembered then having read in the society columns of this daughter, Elaine.

That night Mrs. Beacon brought in our dinner and we ate it by the bedside. When we had finished it was nearly eight o'clock. We ordered Norton Hoorne's car, and, locking the piano, and cautioning the housekeeper to admit no one to the studio in our absence, we drove to the address where lived this girl whose connection with the case appeared so definite, and yet, to us, so unfathomable.

CHAPTER 2

After we had waited perhaps five minutes a young man entered the room, holding in his hand the card Dr. Johns had sent up. He was a few years younger than I—a clean cut, athletic-looking chap—a typical rich man's son of the better sort.

"Won't you sit down, gentlemen?" He waved us back to the chairs from which we had risen, speaking, I thought, in an unnaturally low tone. "I am Mr. Henten—my father is not at home."

"Dr. Manning and myself," Dr. Johns began, when we were seated, glancing at me an instant by way of introduction. "Mr. Henten, we came here this evening to see your father on rather a curious matter. I am sure you will do quite as well."

Our young host inclined his head in agreement and waited.

"I—er—must ask, Mr. Henten, that you will keep all we say strictly confidential?"

The young man nodded gravely.

"Then I will be quite frank with you. I should like to ask first—do you know Norton Hoorne?"

"I have heard of him," said the young man. "I have been to his concerts—he is a very great artist." I thought he spoke a little cautiously, and with a note of coldness in his voice.

"You do not know him personally?"

"I believe—yes, I have met him—some months ago."

Young Mr. Henten seemed to make this admission with reluctance. Then, a little impatiently but without dropping his politely formal manner, he went on—

"But will you tell me what Norton Hoorne—"

"Mr. Henten," Dr. Johns interrupted, "I shall be still more frank with you. We are Norton Hoorne's physicians—and his friends also. Mr. Hoorne is very ill at this moment—very dangerously ill, I might say. This afternoon in his delirium he spoke the name of—er—Miss Henten. There is a photograph of her standing on his desk. From the words he spoke—incoherent—"

The look on the young man's face made Dr. Johns stop abruptly. After an instant he continued, speaking much more firmly than before.

"You will pardon me, Mr. Henten. You must understand we have not the wish—the indelicacy—to pry into Miss Henten's affairs. What we three say here is said in the strictest confidence. We are Mr. Hoorne's physicians. His life is in danger. The information we seek is for his good only. I trust you will understand that and will do what you can to help us."

"What information is it you desire?" asked the young man.

Dr. Johns leaned forward earnestly. "Miss Henten and Norton Hoorne were friends?"

"They were, but the friendship was broken off several months ago."

"Why?"

Young Mr. Henten hesitated. "Elaine was to have married Sir Oliver Baconfield. It was announced recently," he said finally.

"Was to—?"

"My sister died this morning," said the young man quietly.

The effect of this announcement on Dr. Johns and me must have surprised our host greatly.

"Oh, I am very sorry, Mr. Henten," Dr. Johns hastened to say contritely when he had recovered himself somewhat. "I can understand now your reluctance—our coming at such a time—"

The young man bit his lip and looked away; we could see he was struggling to suppress his emotion.

"We will not keep you more than a moment longer," Dr. Johns added. "There are a few questions—I beg you will not think them irrelevant. They have, I assure you, a direct bearing upon Norton Hoorne's present welfare. If you will let me hurt you just a moment more, Mr. Henten. It may be—I think it is—a matter of life or death to our patient."

The young man bowed his head. "What is it you want to know?" he asked in a low voice.

"I will be as brief as possible. Was your sister ever engaged to Norton Hoorne?"

"No—not that I know of."

"They were very good friends?"

"I think so—yes."

"Why was the friendship broken off?"

The young man met Dr. Johns's gaze with a look of almost pleading appeal.

"Why was the friendship broken off?" persisted the doctor. "Did they quarrel?"

"No." The youth spoke so low we could hardly hear him.

"Were they—were they in love?"

Young Mr. Henten's increasing agitation became manifest.

"I'm sorry to hurt you, my lad," Dr. Johns added gently. "But I must know these things. Were they in love?"

"Yes, they were."

"And it was broken off so that she could become engaged to some one else?"

"My—my mother wished her to marry Lord Baconfield. My father forbade her seeing Norton Hoorne again."

Dr. Johns sat back in his chair. "What was the cause of your sister's death, Mr. Henten?" He tried to ask the question quietly, but I knew by my own emotion the anxiety with which he awaited its answer.

Young Mr. Henten raised his head wearily. "She died of pneumonia," he said. "She caught a severe cold. It was very sudden—though she had not been well for some time."

Dr. Johns thought a moment and then resumed.

"After her friendship with Norton Hoorne was broken off, was she—did she seem ill?"

"She never seemed quite herself. She—she—Oh, Dr. Johns, if you please, I—" The young man seemed at the point of breaking down.

"I'm sorry," Dr. Johns said kindly. "If you will just bear with me a moment more—then we will go. Your sister was musical?"

"She would have been a very fine pianist. She was a pupil of Norton Hoorne."

"Afterward—I mean these last few months—did she play frequently?"

"Not as much as before. Only at night sometimes, in the evening, she would go into the music-room alone and play."

"What sort of music would she play?"

"I don't know. It *was* peculiar. Improvisations of her own sometimes, I think. We did not like her to play—it was not good for her."

"Why not?" Dr. Johns's eyes never left the young man's face.

"It made her ill. Once or twice she—she fainted. We found her lying there—once on the floor where she had fallen."

Dr. Johns rose abruptly, and crossing to where the young man sat low down in his chair, laid an arm over his shoulder.

"We will go now, my lad," he said gently. "I am sorry to have hurt you, but it was necessary. I know you do not understand why I have asked these questions. You need never understand—now. And remember—our visit here tonight and what we have said, you have given your promise—you will tell no one?"

"No, sir, I will not mention it, if you wish me not to."

"Thank you." The doctor straightened up. "Your sister was a very fine little woman. You know that—and we know it. Good night, my lad."

"Good night, sir," said the young man, rising.

During the drive back to Norton Hoorne's studio, Dr. Johns showed a peculiar reticence in discussing the interview we had just had. The few questions and comments I volunteered he answered so shortly and with such abstraction of manner that I soon gave up and remained silent.

Back at the house on Riverside Drive, we went immediately to Hoorne's studio. We found nothing unusual had occurred during our absence. Norton Hoorne's body still lay motionless on the cot.

After we had dismissed the housekeeper with such assurances of her master's recovery as we could give, and were again alone, Dr. Johns locked both doors of the room, and turning to face me, began abruptly:

"Will, whatever you or I may think about this case, it is obvious that theoretical discussion of it is futile. I am convinced of but one thing—the secret lies with Norton; we must make him tell us."

"Do we dare?" I asked; I dreaded further musical experiments.

"We must—there is no other way. And to do nothing—" Dr. Johns broke off and shuddered.

"Shall I play now?" I asked. My companion nodded and seated himself beside the cot.

I began to play, softly at first, then louder. For what seemed ages there was no response. Again I heard the sound of that weird voice, babbling incoherently, with low moans, and once interrupted by a piercing shriek.

I ceased playing and heard Dr. Johns say:

"You must speak more clearly, Norton. Now—try—what is it you want to tell us?"

In the silence that followed I played slowly a series of soft modulations. Then I waited, and after a time, from the lips of Norton Hoorne came the words:

"*In the desk—another drawer—the letter—for you. Use it, for God's sake, use it.*"

We found it after a long search, in a secret drawer of the desk. It was a large envelope, sealed, and inscribed with both our names. It contained a folded sheet of music manuscript and a letter. The letter, which was in Hoorne's handwriting, we opened first. It contained only two lines:

I fear this thing. I cannot tell to what it will lead. I know I can trust you both, if need arises, to use the enclosed.

That was all.

The music was written in Hoorne's careless, hurried way, with which I was quite familiar. It was a composition of perhaps sixty bars. And at the top, for its title, was the one word:

"RELEASE"

For a moment we stared at this cryptic paper in silence. Then our glances met, and in Dr. Johns's eyes I read the same doubt of its meaning that he must have seen in mine.

"Can you play it?" he asked; his voice almost broke with the intensity of his emotion.

"Yes," I answered. "Shall I?"

He flung his hands to his head with a gesture of despair.

"Play it," he said hopelessly.

The scene in Norton Hoorne's studio that night, as I remember it, was fantastic and gruesome in the extreme. The room was in semi-darkness. The shades were down, and we had drawn the heavy portières together before the French windows. The corners of the room and its heavily beamed ceiling were shrouded in thick, black shadows. The piano stood quite in shadow, with only a dim glow of amber light from a lamp shining upon its rack and keyboard.

Near by stood the white-linened bed with the ghastly white face of Norton Hoorne upon its snowy pillow. And from a stand at the bedside a beam of light fell full upon the expressionless features.

At first I was trembling so violently I would not dared have made the attempt to play. Forcing myself to calmness, I ran my fingers silently over the keys, staring intently at what I knew instinctively was Hoorne's unplayed composition, finding its extraordinary harmonies, and fixing the rhythm in my mind.

After many minutes of guiding my cold, trembling fingers in their unfamiliar way over the keys, I began to play. In the hush of the room the fantastic music welled out with a throbbing intensity. No longer was I nervous, no longer afraid. The shadows of the studio faded into blackness—a great void of nothingness all about me—as I abandoned myself more and more to the influence of the strange harmonies I was creating. Now my innermost being felt their power, for they awakened emotions my soul had never known before.

The blackness around grew denser. My senses seemed freed of every earthly tie. The room, the piano, everything, was blotted out. Only the music remained, quivering out through the void, crying with the sorrow of the ages, but always tender, inexpressibly tender, and luring—luring me on—and on—

I shall never forget the shock to my senses when the first sharp cry from Dr. Johns brought me to myself. The music died—throbbing away into silence. I found myself sitting at the keyboard, cold and shivering in the hot, close air of the room.

"Look! Look there!" I heard Dr. Johns's low whisper as though from a great distance.

The corner of the room and the ceiling beyond and above Hoorne's white, expressionless face was shrouded with a great, black, grotesque shadow. I do not know what made me stare in that direction, but as I stared the shadow began to take form. At first it seemed merely to waver; then it began to contract, slowly at first, then more rapidly.

Then it seemed no longer black but vaguely luminous, like a silver fog gleaming in the dim light of a hidden moon. And then all at once I realized that it was taking shape. I could see plainly the tiny glowing particles that composed it, twisting and crawling upon themselves. But the shape remained, grew more definite, until at last I recognized it for what it was—the figure of a young girl—the girl of the photograph—the girl whose brother we had just left.

I do not know how long it took me to come to this realization of what I was seeing. Probably it was only an instant; it seemed an eternity.

I could hear Dr. Johns's labored breathing—see dimly the outlines of the cot and Hoorne's face upon its pillow. But all that remained clear and real was the figure of this girl, quivering there in the air above the bed.

The upper part of her body particularly was vivid; below the breasts it seemed to melt away into the blackness of the room beyond. Her hair hung in two flowing braids over her bare shoulders; her arms were reaching down toward the bed, and on her beautiful face was a look of tenderness and sorrow and unutterable longing.

And then I saw that around her head and shoulders there hung another radiance, dimmer far than the outlines of her form—a radiance that seemed to fade away as I looked at it directly. Yet I knew it was there; and I seemed to feel, too, rather than see, that it was not silver, but the delicate color of a rose—a color extraordinarily beautiful, yet fragile, wistful as the rose petals it resembled.

Then as I sat staring I heard a whisper come up from the bed. The whisper grew louder, and I heard that same toneless voice from the lips of Norton Hoorne, saying:

"I cannot stay here. I must go. Play—play—you must play."

I think I must have resumed playing; I know I heard music—the same music as before, only softer, sweeter, more tender.

And then, from the body lying inert on the bed, I saw issue another shape—in outline, form, and every detail the body of Norton Hoorne. It glowed, swirled, and drifted upward. It was Norton Hoorne—its face the face of my friend as I had always known him. After an instant his figure hung swaying above the bed. And from it depended a thin silver cord—fine as the finest gossamer, holding it chained to its human shell below.

The music swelled louder. The arms of the girl reached out; her eyes seemed to cry aloud with yearning. The man's figure pulled and strained at its leash, but the silver cord held strong.

The music grew still louder, thundering now in the hush of the room. The body in the bed sat up suddenly, beating with clenched hands its naked breast. And then, slowly it seemed, the silver cord parted.

A look of ineffable happiness suffused the girl's face as the man's figure, growing suddenly brighter, swirled upward and mingled with hers.

The body on the bed fell back upon the pillow and lay motionless. The mingled shapes above drifted away. The music ceased abruptly.

Norton Hoorne was—dead?

www.ingramcontent.com/pod-product-compliance
Lightning Source LLC
Chambersburg PA
CBHW020655180626
46816CB00003B/1287